HAPPY BIRTHDAY
JESUS

To Ray

HAPPY BIRTHDAY JESUS

A Novel

C.C. Risenhoover

McLennan HOUSE
WAXAHACHIE

Published by
McLennan House, Inc.
206 South Rogers
Waxahachie, Texas 75165

Copyright © 1986 by C.C. Risenhoover

All rights reserved. No part of this book may be reproduced
or transmitted in any form or by any means, electronic or
mechanical, including photocopying, recording or by any information storage and retrieval system, without the written per-
mission of the publisher, except when permitted by law.

Library of Congress Cataloging-in-Publication Data

Risenhoover, C.C., 1936–
HAPPY BIRTHDAY JESUS

I. Title
ISBN 0–918865–06–9
Library of Congress Catalog Number: 86–62296

Manufactured in the United States of America
First Printing

Christ came to us bringing peace, love, joy, laughter, and healing. When he returns again, he will lead his disciples in a chorus of laughter, because as the old saying goes, the Devil can't stand the sound of laughter. Christ will lead the disciples, the wounded and the broken-hearted, in laughing away all the hypocrites, the greedy, the cruel, and all those who think they can hurt other people and get away with it. We will all join Christ in laughing away the false doctrines and pompous theories of our times. He will help us laugh away our despair, our hatred, our vindictiveness, fear, anxiety, and depression, and all the things that make people sick in their souls. He will laugh away the barriers among Christians and between Christians and unbelievers. All will be blown away with divine laughter.

from **THE JOYFUL CHRIST: THE
HEALING POWER OF HUMOR**
by Cal Samara
(Harper & Row, 1986)

I

I actually met the man who called himself Jesus on a Sunday, December Seventh, at about nine-thirty in the evening. The memory of that meeting is quite vivid to me because of numerous factors, not the least of which was the man himself.

As I recall, I was stationed on a barstool at an eating and drinking establishment located on Preston and just off the LBJ Freeway. You might say that I was crying in my beer, though that is figuratively speaking. In truth, I was drinking margaritas at a fairly rapid clip, feeling sorry for myself because my heart had been broken by some wench whose name I no longer remember.

There weren't many people in the bar area, which is not unusual for a Sunday night. I suspect most people go to bed early Sunday night in order to be fresh for work Monday morning. But, fortunately or unfortunately, I work for a newspaper and my hours are somewhat flexible.

Anyway, as previously stated, I was lamenting my most recent dumping by someone of the female gender, getting angrier by the moment. Expletives were dancing like sugar plums in my brain, though I haven't the foggiest idea as to what a sugar plum looks like. Many of us who were reared in Texas don't know much about sugar plums or roasting chestnuts on an open fire, though both sound nice in poem or song.

I mention the above only because the Christmas season was in full swing, at least from a marketing standpoint. Even the bar was displaying its usual MERRY XMAS signs.

Rejection is not easy to take, but I wouldn't want you to think that the dumping by ol' what's her name caused any tears on my part. I cried when my bird dog died, but am not likely to dispense tears as the result of getting the heave-ho from some air-headed chick. Still, I was sad, which is more than sufficient reason for a few extra margaritas.

I've since wondered if there is any significance to having met the man who called himself Jesus on December Seventh, but don't really think so. For me, the date will continue to live in infamy only because of the Japanese bombing of Pearl Harbor.

As I recall, the cold of winter had seemingly set in, though Texas weather can be as temperamental as a woman who is surprised to learn that she has exceeded the limit on her MasterCard or Visa. The temperature was hovering around thirty degrees and the north wind had pushed the chill factor down around zero. The previous day had been a complete contradiction, with a warm southerly wind blowing in from the Gulf of Mexico and bringing with it all sorts of wonderful pollen for the nostrils of those subject to allergies.

Unfortunately, I'm one of those who attracts allergies like Texas attracts illegal aliens, which seems to range in the millions. I had only recently spent considerable money on allergy treatments or my head might have been hurting worse than it did. As it was, it felt like a basketball must feel when dribbled on a concrete court.

It's a good thing allergy doctors don't have to guarantee their work. It's a good thing a lot of us don't have to guarantee our work.

There was no way I was going to blame my headache on the margarita setting in front of me, or on the others I'd already consumed. Margaritas have a healing effect, especially on allergies that cause a stuffy head and runny nose. Take an order of beef nachos covered with jalapeno peppers, wash it down with a few margaritas, and you have a cure for just about anything that ails you.

Including a broken heart.

At least that's what I thought at the time.

Anyway, when the man who called himself Jesus walked through the door, I was nursing a margarita and contemplating my good looks in the mirror behind the bar. The only problem with the mirror is that it has all this scribbly stuff all over it. I don't know the proper name for the scribbly stuff, but you know what I mean.

There isn't, however, enough scribbly stuff to hide the crookedness of my nose, the result of a misspent youth trying to prove myself in Golden Gloves competition. Also easy enough to see is the gray hair, the lines in the face and the bags under the eyes.

If the bags get any worse, I figure airlines will soon have me checking them in when I take a flight. I'm just glad that the bar hides my paunch from the mirror.

Age is doing its thing, taking its toll.

The man who called himself Jesus walked right up to where I was sitting, interrupted my thoughts by asking if I'd mind if he sat on the stool beside me. Because there were only three other persons in the place, none other than me sitting at the bar, my guard went up. After all, Dallas is allegedly second only to San Francisco in the number of fag residents, all acting as though they have a right to have and spread AIDS. They're as vehement about their right to disease as those of us in the National Rifle Association are about our right to have and bear arms.

If you didn't know better, you'd think AIDS was a political party.

I looked into the man's eyes, though, and immediately decided he was straight arrow. His eyes looked honest and true, not shifty like an editor's or publisher's. And because of the kindness and softness I saw in his eyes, I knew he couldn't be a doctor, lawyer or banker.

Because the man was dressed in generic attire,

an obviously off-the-rack suit and nondescript tie, I figured him for a laborer of some type, out for a few beers and with hopes of meeting a broad.

He shocked me when he stuck out a hand and said, "My name's Jesus."

I shook the extended hand, chuckled, perhaps a bit nervously, and replied, "Of course it is."

"I'm serious."

"And I'm the apostle Peter."

He smiled and said, "No, your name's Mark Luther."

Suspiciously, I asked, "How did you know that?"

"I know quite a bit about you."

The gears started turning in my mind, and I glanced furtively about the place, thinking I might see one of my alleged friends.

Alleged is one of my favorite words, one of the reasons I went into journalism instead of brain surgery.

A number of my alleged friends spend considerable time and expense trying to screw up my mind, a difficult task at best. It's practically impossible to warp something that is already severely bent.

Though the man didn't look Mexican, I said, "You say your name is Jesus. You'd normally pronounce it Hay-suice, wouldn't you?"

"No, it's pronounced Geez-us."

While not into irreverence, I decided to go along with the gag. "You mean as in the Son of God?"

"The same."

"If I were you, pal, I'd be careful of lightning bolts. Who sent you here? Was it Bobby Jack? Joe Don? Billy Bob?"

"None of your friends sent me here."

"How do you know the guys I named are my friends?"

"Like I told you, I know a lot about you."

Let me emphasize that there was no arrogance in the man. He was soft-spoken, seemingly self-assured, and with a very calm demeanor.

I laughed. "Well, if you're who you say you are, welcome back to earth."

"What makes you think I just arrived?"

"Sorry, I just assumed. Would you like a drink?"

"I'll take a glass of water."

I grinned. "That's right, you can turn it into wine if you like."

He looked bemused. "I'm surprised that you remember any scripture. You haven't exactly been a pillar of the church for the past few years."

"I kind of gave it up after I got out of the cookies and Kool-Aid stage."

"Yes, I know."

I signaled the bartender, asked him to bring me another margarita and a glass of water for the man who called himself Jesus. Then I said, "A man doesn't forget scripture. I can recite the Twenty-third Psalm and the Lord's Prayer."

"I'm impressed," he said.

"You should be."

Those more spiritual than me always talk about having had some unique religious experience during which Jesus came into their heart. This man who called himself Jesus hadn't come into my heart, but he had come into my favorite bar.

There was a time in my youth, during Vacation Bible School, when I allegedly took Christ as my personal savior. The inner feelings I had during that period of time have long since escaped my memory. I can only recall that with cookies and Kool-Aid some well-meaning persons induced me into making a commitment, and I was later baptized. This is not a criticism of those providing the cookies, Kool-Aid and religious counsel, merely testimony that I was easily persuaded.

When the bartender returned with the margarita and the water, I suggested, "Why don't you turn that water into wine?"

He laughed and said, "I could probably do you a good deed by turning that margarita into water."

"That sure would be a waste, but fire away. If you could do it, it would help prove you're who you claim to be."

"I don't need to prove anything."

Sarcastically, I said, "That's what I figured." But when I took a sip of my drink, I did a doubletake because it tasted exactly like water. Good water, too. The only thing was, it still looked like a frozen margarita. I sampled it again and got the same taste results.

"That's a good trick," I admitted. "How did you do it?"

"Do what?"

"Make my drink taste like water."

"Maybe it's just your imagination."

"Have it your way," I said, then summoned the bartender and continued, "Sorry, pal, but this margarita tastes just like water. Would you mind fixing me another?"

The bartender looked at the glass curiously, took a sip and said, "It sure tastes like a margarita to me."

"It sure looks like a margarita," I agreed, "but it doesn't taste like one to me. Just get me another. I'll pay for it."

"No, you don't have to pay," the bartender said, "I'll get you one on the house."

After he had left to fix the drink, I turned to my companion and said, "Okay, I'm watching you all the way this time. No tricks with this drink."

"I don't do tricks."

"Well, if you can turn this next drink into water, then I may start believing you're who you say you are."

"If that's what it takes to get you to believe, then you'll just have to remain an unbeliever."

"Don't get touchy. I'm sure you already know I'm a skeptic and cynic."

"Yes, I do know," he said, "And I'm sure you think that such traits make you a better journalist."

"They can't hurt."

"Are you sure about that?"

The bartender had returned with my margarita, which I hadn't allowed out of my sight, even while he was building it. I took a sip and again it tasted like water. I couldn't even taste the salt around the rim of the glass.

"Look, whoever you are," I said to my companion, "I don't know what kind of conspiracy's going on here, but enough's enough. The joke's over."

He chuckled and said, "I didn't know there was a joke."

"This drink's a joke, so I have to assume the bartender is in on the deal with you."

"Please don't get upset," he said.

"I'm going to call the bartender back over here, and if he doesn't give me a real drink, I may shove this one down his throat. Or down yours."

"Don't call the bartender. Try your drink again."

I tasted again, and it was pure margarita.

"How in the . . ."

"Don't ask," he said.

"Well, I have to hand it to you. It's one of the best magic acts I've ever seen."

"There is no magic," he assured.

I snorted. "You're quite a humorist."

"In your perception of religion, you don't allow for Jesus, or God, to have a sense of humor, do you?"

"I've never given it much thought, but I wish you wouldn't come on with that religious act. It makes me a bit nervous."

"My presence usually makes people nervous."

"I'd say that's a problem you ought to work on."

"I can only be who I am."

"I don't know who you are, pal, but if some of my friends have paid you to do this act, it's the most distasteful they've ever been."

"Why?"

"C'mon, pretending to be the Son of God. That's pretty low."

He chuckled. "Since you don't claim to be a religious man, I don't see why religious claims, by anyone, should bother you."

The margaritas had made my mind a bit fuzzy, but like most drunks, I still figured I had complete control of all my faculties. "Just because I'm not a church-goer doesn't mean I don't believe in God."

"What does believing in God mean to you?"

"It means a lot of stuff, more than I care to relate."

"When you can honestly answer my question, there might be some hope for you."

"Boy, what does that mean?"

"It means that you have to be honest with yourself."

What I couldn't understand was my willingness to listen to the fraud sitting beside me, yet for some reason I was genuinely intrigued with his claims and our conversation. There was something about him that was so different it was frightening. It was as though he could look right into my soul. In my wildest dreams, I never imagined sitting in a bar on a Sunday night discussing religion with a man who claimed to be the Son of God.

Maybe I was drunker than I thought.

"Since you're obviously not going to be truthful with me, and since I've always wanted to find out a few things from God, I'm going to go along with you being who you say you are," I said. "That way, we can at least make this conversation a little more interesting."

"Oh," he replied, "if I'm boring you, I can leave."

"No, don't leave. Do you want another glass of water, or maybe something stronger?"

"I'm fine."

I ordered another margarita, then asked, "Why would Jesus Christ want to visit Dallas, Texas?"

"I don't know that it's a matter of wanting to visit any particular place," he said. "It's here, so I'm here."

"There's nothing to do here," I said, "nothing to do but shop. We have lots of places to shop. But I guess you know that, you being omnipresent and all."

I was beginning to get in the swing of things, so I asked, "Why did you come to see me? Did you think I might get you a little press?"

He laughed, "I hardly think you could get me any press."

"Hey, don't sell me short," I said. "I might be

able to get your visit in the *National Inquirer.* It would make a pretty good headline, JESUS VISITS REPORTER. Yeah, it's the stuff a good *Inquirer* story is made of."

"You're assuming I'm in Dallas just to see you."

"Why shouldn't I assume it? My friends didn't pay you to visit with someone else, too, did they?"

Again, he chuckled. "You are a hard case, Mark."

"Damn right."

"Well, you are right about one thing. I did specifically want to make myself known to you."

"Great," I said. "Ask anything of me and I'll do it."

"Why would you do that?"

"Maybe because I'm afraid of God."

"You're being facetious, but you've brought up a major problem. A lot of people are afraid of God."

I grunted. "I guess they have good cause to be."

"What most people attribute to God is man's inhumanity to man. God's not cruel."

"I didn't know I was going to end up debating religion with some clown tonight, but since we're into it, I think I can give you a run for your money. This inhumanity you talk about, why doesn't God stop it? He could, couldn't He?"

"Of course, if he wanted to make men robots. He could make you sexless, mindless . . . make you nothing more than a mechanical device who would never get hungry, angry, sad or show any type emotion. Instead, He gave you a free will, made choice available to you. It's one of the most difficult things for a man to understand."

"You're saying God doesn't have any control over a man's life," I argued.

"That's right."

I frowned. "I don't think that's theologically sound."

"Believe me, it's sound," the man said. "Of course, Mark, you're like most people. You want to believe God controls your life so you'll have someone to blame for the wrong that happens in it."

"That's not true."

"Isn't it? A person who credits God for all the good in his life tends to also blame Him for everything that goes wrong."

"You're saying God doesn't intervene in the affairs of man, which just doesn't make sense to me," I said.

"What you call intervention is man choosing to follow the dictates or example of God. It still comes down to a matter of choice. A man controls his own life, especially his relationship to God."

"If that's the case, what point is there in prayer?"

"Prayer is communion with God, a reassurance of salvation. What is asked for in prayer should be precipitated by a willingness to follow God's directives. In doing that, a man's prayers are answered.

"For example, if you pray that hungry children

in the world will be fed, you can have that prayer answered by giving your money for that purpose. God's already told you what is important in life, so in prayer you have a chance to talk things over with God and do what's right. Prayer is not just two-way communication, it's also two-way participation. If you're committed to God, He uses all your senses to do His work on earth."

Maybe it was the way the guy talked, maybe it was the booze, but I was in a dreamy state, remembering everything he said and wanting more.

"What you're saying is that I shouldn't ask God for a million dollars."

He shook his head, not in response to my statement but in resignation and said, "If you want to pray for a million dollars, feel free. Your prayer might even be answered, if you're willing to properly commit your time, energies and abilities to that goal. But God doesn't deal in the monetary. He deals in the spiritual."

"So, how come every time I go to church the preacher is harping about money?"

"For one thing, what you say isn't true. You haven't made a nusiance of yourself at church, but most of the time when you've been there money hasn't been mentioned. It does take money to operate a church, but there's an even stronger motivational factor for giving."

"What's that?"

"Where your treasure is, that's where your

heart's going to be."

"It seems I remember a scripture like that."

He laughed. "Yeah, I did say something along those lines, but I'm surprised you'd remember it."

"You seem to have a pretty low opinion of me."

"Quite the contrary. While I do know your imperfections, I also realize your potential. If I were picking apostles again, you'd have a shot at being one."

"You're crazy, you know that?"

"That seems to have been the consensus when I was first sent to earth, and while many have embraced the idea of Christianity, very few have embraced my way."

"What do you mean?"

"I mean that most people think of being a Christian in the same way they think of being a Democrat or Republican," he said, "or being a member of a country club or service organization."

"I'll bet you're a preacher," I said, "and from the way you're dressed, I'd have to guess you're a country preacher."

"I consider myself more as a teacher, but I'm also Jesus Christ," he said.

I ignored the latter part of his statement and said, "You know, a person who had a tremendous affect on my life was a country preacher. He was a good man, really helped me through some hard times."

"Yes, I know," the stranger said, "But you've obviously filed all the spiritual help you received away to where it's no longer a bother to you. You don't want the spiritual to interfere with the way you've chosen to live your life."

He was getting on my nerves a bit, so I retorted, "I'll have you know I'm not the worst guy around. I care about people, spiritual things. I've even been thinking about making a monthly commitment to the *Save The Children Fund*."

"Well, thinking about it certainly isn't going to cost you anything."

It was a good shot, and it hurt. But I figured I'd been playing defense long enough, that I needed to go on the offensive.

"Where had you been before coming in here to interrupt my evening?" I asked.

He sighed. "I went to church."

"Which one? Baptist? Catholic? Methodist? I've always wanted to know which church Jesus would choose."

"Denominations are man's work, not God's," he said. "Again, man should choose the church or group he thinks coincides closest with my way."

"So you're not going to tell me where you went?"

"No, but I'll tell you that I was disappointed."

"You must have known you'd be disappointed before you went, being all knowing like you are."

"We won't get into that, but the building and many of the people were so ostentatious, the service such a production geared to stirring emotions totally unrelated to Christianity, that I almost puked."

I chuckled. "I could have told you the churches in this town are full of hypocrites."

He came back, "The hypocrites in church have a better chance of finding the truth than the hypocrites outside it."

I knew I'd been hit with another good shot, but undaunted asked, "Why didn't you cleanse the temple, throw all those ostentatious folks out of it?"

He gave me an incredulous look and said, "I don't think you'll understand this, but that building where I went to church has nothing to do with me or my way. This bar can be as holy a place as the building where I went to church. The buildings where people go to church, all the elaborate furnishings in them, the stained glass windows, they all belong to man and are for the glory of man. The only thing that belongs to God, the only thing God treasures, is the individual commitment he receives from a believer."

"Well, I've always said too much money is wasted on church buildings."

"Too much money is wasted on everything," he said. "But what you want to do is classify all churches as bad, and that just isn't true. Some are nothing more than financial rackets, with all assets vested in the name of the pastors, but you can find a good church, if you're interested in finding one. Just be sure you're searching for truth, not for people and doctrine to feed your prejudices.

"One of the great untruths in the world is to say that one church is as good as another. That's absurd. Unfortunately, men have to judge churches, and sometimes that judgment can be mistaken and imperfect. But the refusal to judge is manifestly worse."

To my way of thinking, the guy had made a mistake with the aforementioned statement, and I was quick to point it out. "I thought you said something about not judging, that you be not judged."

He smiled. "It's good to know that some of your days in church weren't wasted. What Matthew attributed to me was, *Judge not, that you be not judged. For with the judgment you pronounce you will be judged.* Matthew reported my words correctly, but what he didn't say was that I was using irony to get across my point. The intended implication is the exact opposite of the literal sense. I was not making a categorical command never to render judgment. If obeyed, a command like that would destroy all that is best in human life. I was warning that if you want to avoid judgment on yourself, you have to do the impossible, which is to refuse to engage in any judgment at all."

I peered at what was left of my margarita, decided this guy was deep, even for me. You see, I kind of pride myself on my intelligence. I have a pretty high IQ.

He continued, "If you give up judgment, you give up almost everything that dignifies human life. You're forced to make judgments every day, almost every moment of your life. Again, I stress that God gives you the opportunity to choose, to judge."

"If what you say is true, a lot of what I've been hearing in church over the years is untrue," I said.

"As I previously related, man's church is not necessarily God's church," he said. "God's church is spiritual, whereas man is incapable of keeping materialism out of his church. The true church is an idea for which individually committed people strive as a collective force."

I grunted, "The way you put it, it's impossible to have a true church. I'm not into impossible goals."

"Why not? Impossible goals are what makes life worth living. If your only goals in life can be easily achieved, you're missing the really high calling. A man shouldn't be content with imperfection simply because he considers perfection unobtainable."

"I don't think many people are going to buy that kind of deal," I said.

"You're right. Not many will make the commitment to follow my way."

Maybe the margaritas had dulled my senses, because when the man said he was going to have to find a room for the night, that there were no vacancies at the Valley View Inn, I suddenly found myself inviting him to spend the night at my place.

When we left the bar, the cold air wasn't enough to sober me, so he took it on himself to handle the driving. He didn't bother to ask directions, just started the car and took the shortest route to my house.

II

The next morning I awoke to the aroma of frying bacon and freshly brewed coffee. After robing and houseshoeing myself, I staggered into the bathroom and, with cold water, washed the sleep from my eyes. I also checked myself in the mirror to see if my head was as big and ugly as it felt.

Ugh!

The head looked normal-size. As for the ugly, all the soap and water in the world can't wash that away. As always, after a stupid bout with alcohol, I was mentally repentant and determined to change my lifestyle.

The man who claimed to be Jesus was sitting at the breakfast table, reading the newspaper, a mug filled with coffee cradled in his right hand.

He glanced up from the paper and asked, "How do you want your eggs?"

I groaned. "I don't. What time is it?"

"It's six o'clock."

"My god, it's still night."

He laughed. "You need to be up and about."

"Why?"

"Getting started early in the morning is good for the soul."

"Maybe that's been my problem all these years. Anything interesting in the paper?" I was still wondering why I had invited this man to come home with me. I'm normally not so trusting, but for some reason felt I had nothing to fear from him.

"Your DART board is still bickering," he said.

The reference was to *Dallas Area Rapid Transit,* a local government group put together for the purpose of providing public transportation in and around Dallas. The whole project is nothing more than a political football. The entire doomed-to-failure operation is one of my pet peeves.

"That's not news," I said. "All they do is bicker, and for what? Dallas doesn't need mass transit. It's not like New York City."

He shrugged his shoulders and said, "Hey, I'm not responsible for DART."

I laughed. "Are you denying that God has anything to do with DART? It would make a good story for the paper."

"I don't have any problem with that denial," he said.

I poured myself a cup of coffee and sat down at the table. "I meant to ask how you got to the bar last night. Did one of my friends drop you?"

"No, to tell the truth, I rode a DART bus."

"Wasn't it lonely?"

He chuckled. "Well, other than the driver, I was the only person on the bus."

"A friend of mine recently saw four people on a DART bus and got all excited about the bus carrying such a crowd, but he later discovered the driver was just taking his family on an outing."

The man smiled. "The DART situation really gets you agitated, doesn't it?"

"You could say that. The interior of a DART bus is the most private place you can find in Dallas. Practically no one rides the buses, so the DART board can't wait to go out and spend millions buying bigger buses. Now they're planning to spend billions on a rail service that no one will ride."

"If you don't approve of what they're doing, why don't you do something about it?"

"Like what?"

"What about the power of the press?"

"It's kind of hard to get the paper up in arms about DART, since someone keeps saying 'Everyone knows Dallas needs a mass transit system.' Of course, everyone doesn't know it, but that's the big lie being perpetrated. Besides, DART spends a lot of money advertising in the paper and with other media. That's the best way to keep the media quiet."

"So, you just gripe and don't try to do anything about it."

I took a swig of coffee, then said, "Hey, man, I'm not like you claim to be. I don't have any power from on high. The big problem is Dallas traffic. What would you do about it if you were in charge?"

He got up from the table, poured himself another cup of coffee and returned. "Speaking strictly from a common sense standpoint," he said, "I'd insist that road construction work be done at night, not when traffic is at its peak. I'd also start a campaign to teach people how they should drive. And I'd make it illegal for an off-duty policeman, for anyone, to direct traffic on public streets for the benefit of private business."

To say I liked and approved of what he said would be an understatement. It's what I'd been preaching to anyone who would listen.

"If drivers would plan their trips, take right turns instead of left turns against three lanes of oncoming traffic, the traffic situation would be smoother," he continued. "The city also needs to get rid of left turns into shopping centers where there is no traffic light. It would be better for one driver to go a little out of his or her way rather than to inconvenience a hundred drivers."

"Amen," I said.

"You like what I've said, huh?"

"I sure do. It's what I've been saying for some time."

He sighed. "I know, but you haven't been getting your message to the right people."

"Well, I've been thinking about writing some editorials."

He laughed. "Thinking about it shouldn't take up too much of your valuable time."

"Hey, wait a minute. If you know my thoughts on DART and Dallas' traffic problems, you've been talking to my friends."

"No, but I would like to meet your friends."

"Yeah, how am I going to introduce you? By what name?"

"Just introduce me as Jesus."

"Sure, and you can introduce me as crazy."

He got up, brought the coffee pot to the table and filled my cup. "Don't get overwrought. Your friends might be more accepting of me than you are."

I laughed. "If you think that, maybe you don't know my friends. If I was going to introduce you to them, I'd just call you J.C. Yeah, that's a good name for you . . . J.C. Smith."

"You Southerners have always liked initials," he said.

My guard went up. "You don't like the South?"

"I have nothing against the South," he said with a chuckle. "The South, and Southerners, have some redeeming qualities."

"Well, I don't guess you would have been on our side during the Civil War."

"War is man's idea, not God's. It's just another choice man makes."

He picked up a crisp piece of bacon and began to munch on it.

"Aha," I said, "if you're who you say you are, you wouldn't be eating that bacon."

"Why not?"

"Because you're Jewish, orthodox I'd guess."

He laughed. "I'm not Jewish."

"Well, when Jesus came to earth, he came as a Jew. The Jews are God's chosen people."

"That's ridiculous. God doesn't choose a people. A person chooses God."

"What about Moses?"

"What about him?"

"God chose him to lead the Jews out of bondage."

"Moses chose God, then sought and followed God's directives," he said. "Moses made a commitment to God's Way."

"When the real Jesus came to earth, he came as a Jew," I argued.

The man shrugged his shoulders. "It was a matter of coming into the most appropriate culture of the time. God could just as easily have sent me as an Ethiopian, even as an American if this culture had been functional at the time. I'm universal, not ethnic."

"Man, I wish you'd quit saying stuff like that."

"Why, it's true?"

"It's just not right, a man claiming to be the Son of God in order to play a gag."

"I keep telling you it's not a gag, that I am the Son of God," he said. "Why is it so hard for you to believe me?"

"Well, for one thing, if the Son of God was going to show up in Dallas, Texas, I don't think he'd be hanging out with me."

"Why, because you're not a righteous man? Prior to being crucified, I was accused of hanging out with a lot of bad characters. If you'll remember, I came to bring hope to sinners, not to the righteous."

"I'll give you credit for this," I said, "you are a smooth talker. And you seem to know the Bible backwards and forwards. But man, I still get nervous about the way you're coming on. It has to be blasphemy."

He laughed. "What do you really know about blasphemy? Most of those accusing others of it are themselves blasphemous to the core. Of course, I'm not surprised you would accuse me of blasphemy against God, since I've always been accused of it."

"You're good, really good," I said. "You don't let your guard down, do you?"

"You say I don't let my guard down, but what about you, Mark? You have to keep your guard up constantly because of the things in life that you think are important."

"What do you know about the things I think are important? You have no idea."

"Why don't you tell me what you think is important, what you want from life? I'd like to see if you can tell me without lying, to me and to yourself."

Why the guy wasn't getting on my nerves, I didn't know. I just knew that he was interesting, that I was enjoying talking with him. "It's no secret as to what I want in life," I said. "I want a wife, children, a nice home, a job making enough money to be comfortable on."

He chuckled at my revelation. "I hope you don't believe the lie you just told me."

"It's not a lie."

"Mark, your entire interest in life is sex and money. In fact, the only reason you want more money is because you think it'll help you with your sex life."

"I don't need that much help with it."

"I agree," he said, "but you do need a lot of help when it comes to honesty. You've hurt a lot of people along the way, including a lot of young women who believed your lies."

"I've been hurt a little myself."

"I can't deny that, but you can't do much about being hurt. You can do something about hurting others."

I grunted. "Is this where we start talking about what is and isn't sin?"

"You need to try to overcome your self-centeredness," he said. "For that matter, you need to try to overcome your sex-centeredness."

"I've been called a lot of things, but never sex-centered."

"Just because no one has called your attention to it doesn't mean it isn't so," he said. "Would you deny that you spend an inordinate amount of time thinking about women, about having sex with different women?"

"I don't know what's inordinate," I grumbled. I wanted to be mad because he was hitting below the belt, but it was hard to be angry at the truth.

"At one time you had a fine wife, one who loved you very much," he said. "You weren't faithful to her for even a year. So far, you haven't proved yourself capable of being faithful to any woman."

The fact that I'd been unfaithful to my wife in the very first year of our marriage was something I didn't think anyone knew, even my ex-wife. It was something I wasn't proud of, something I hadn't discussed with anyone. The only way this guy could have found out about it, I thought, was from the woman with whom I'd been unfaithful. And I really didn't think she had been going around bragging about it.

"I don't know where you get your material," I said, "but it's erroneous."

"Are you going to sit there and tell me you weren't unfaithful to your wife?"

I got up from the chair and said, "I'm not going to tell you anything. I'm going to take a couple of Extra Strength Excedrins, because I have a bad headache."

He laughed. "I told you the margaritas would get you."

"Yeah, I know. You told me." I got a couple of Excedrins from the bottle in the kitchen cabinet and downed them with a shot of water. "What do you plan to do today?" I asked.

"I plan to go out and try to find a job and a place to live," he said.

"What kind of job?"

"Anything. I'd like to find a place that would let me work for room and board."

I got another cup of coffee and sat back down. "You're obviously an educated man. You can do better than a job for room and board."

He smiled. "I'm not educated in the sense you're talking about," he said. "I don't have a degree from anywhere, not even from an elementary school."

"C'mon, where did you go to school? Baylor? SMU? TCU?"

"Why would I have gone to any of those schools?"

"Well, they're Christian schools."

He gave a booming laugh.

I couldn't help but laugh with him. "I didn't mean to be humorous. Seriously, where did you go to school?"

"If you want to call it school, I suppose I went at the place you call Heaven."

"Hey, can't you be serious for just a minute?"

"I am serious. I can't make you believe anything other than what you want to believe, though."

The man was a real enigma, but I was still convinced he was carrying out a charade orchestrated by some of my friends. All the time I was talking to him, I was trying to come up with a way to get even with the clowns who were trying to put one over on me. Except I didn't know who they were.

As to why I volunteered the following, I don't know, but I heard myself saying, "You're welcome to stay here while you're looking for a job."

"I don't want to be a bother."

"You won't be. There's plenty of room." I have a three-bedroom house, much bigger than I need. But it comes in handy when my children come to visit. And it's not bad for entertaining a lady now and then. There's a hot tub built into the deck.

"If I stay, I'll do the housework and cooking," he said. "I can be your servant."

"Hey, c'mon, I don't need or want a servant. You're just welcome to stay, if you like."

"We can try it," he said. "If you get uneasy with the situation, just tell me and I'll leave."

"You won't bother me," I said. "Just don't preach to me and everything will be okay."

"I'm afraid I can't make that promise."

"Okay, so don't make it. I sure don't have to listen to you. I just hope you'll let me know who put you up to all this before long."

He sighed. "I keep telling you that no one put me up to anything."

"And I keep telling you that I know when someone is putting me on. Regardless, if you're who you say you are, there's a lot of building going on in this area. Maybe you can get a job as a carpenter. This is a right-to-work state. You don't need a union card."

"It might be a little difficult," he said with a smile, "since I don't even have a Social Security Card."

"That doesn't seem to hinder all the illegal aliens from getting jobs with construction crews," I said.

"The difference is that I can't lie," he said.

There was something in his eyes that told me what he said was the truth, but I didn't want to believe it. "If you can't lie, you're in for some tough sledding," I said.

"Think about it," he said. "What kind of job can the Son of God get in your society?"

I shrugged my shoulders. "I guess you could be pastor of a church."

He shook his head. "I can preach, but what church would really want me? I'd be a problem for any church."

"If you were going to pastor some churches, you'd need some new threads, that's for sure."

"There are a few other things I'd need, too," he said. "I'd need college and seminary degrees, I'd need a wife, I'd need experience."

"If you think you'd need a wife, I don't guess you're Catholic."

He sighed. "I'm only mentioning some of the negatives associated with a composite group of churches, not a specific church. Besides, I consider myself more a teacher than a preacher. John the Baptist, now he was a preacher."

"Hey, I'm not the one who devised the system," I said. "It's my understanding that every church is supposedly built on God's Word, or what some folks thought was God's Word."

"I'm just trying to get you to think of where the Son of God would fit in this society," he said.

"It's something to ponder," I said, "but right now I'm going to shower and shave."

By the time I had finished showering and shaving, I was questioning my invitation to the man who claimed to be the Son of God. However, I decided there wasn't much to worry about. He would soon tire of his act and go on his way, or my friends would tire of paying him. An actor of his ability had to be demanding a tidy sum. I hoped my protagonist, singular or plural, was having to pay through the nose.

But what still baffled me was my willingness to listen so intently to the man who called himself Jesus, to even solicit his words and opinions. He was, indeed, a knowledgeable fellow, but I was not one to put up with a phony act for long. Not normally.

It was only seven-thirty when I finished dressing, which was far earlier than I usually challenged Dallas traffic. However, since I was up and about I called Mary Lou Magruder and asked her to meet me for breakfast at Walls Deli.

En route to the breakfast rendezvous, several DART buses got in my way. All were relatively empty of passengers, which didn't surprise me. The presence of the buses did make me angry because the city was having budget problems, and DART was siphoning our tax money like a thirsty bull at a water hole.

My feeling is that if mass transit is viable, private sources will fund and operate it. With the money DART plans to spend over the next few years, the city could pick up cab fare for anyone in the area who needs a ride for the next century.

I decided Jesus would agree with me, then angrily thought, I've got to quit thinking of that guy as Jesus.

I had entrenched myself in a booth and was working on a second cup of coffee when Mary Lou entered the deli. She is quite an eyeful, tall and willowy, with auburn hair, a ready smile and a wit that is the equal of anyone I've ever met. There was a time when I thought I was in love with her, but it was simply a matter of lust.

The man who called himself Jesus had seen right through me on that score.

"This is quite a surprise," Mary Lou said, seating herself across from me. "I haven't seen the great Mark Luther this early in the morning for quite some time."

I grinned. "Hey, I've decided to make early to bed and early to rise a habit. I've been told it's good for the soul."

"If that's the case, it's a resolution you should abide by."

The waitress brought Mary Lou some coffee and

asked if we were ready to order. Mary Lou ordered bacon, eggs and pancakes, and I ordered one scrambled egg with toast. Mary Lou's ex-husband once said she ate like a bird. He had obviously watched some big birds eat during his lifetime, because Mary Lou can out-eat and out-drink any woman I know.

"So," she said with a smile, after the waitress was out of earshot, "to what do I owe this honor?"

"Can't I just call and ask you to breakfast sometime without wanting something?"

"You could, but you never have."

"That's not true. We've shared a lot of mornings together when I didn't want anything."

"I thought we were going to share a lifetime of them."

"Maybe we should have, but the timing was all wrong."

She shrugged her shoulders. "How is Carole?"

Carole is my ex-wife, mother of my two children. When a woman I'm dating closes in on me, I've often used Carole to get out of the situation. Carole doesn't know it, of course, but I've broken off with more than one young lady by telling her I was going back to Carole. I used the Carole line on Mary Lou, but she saw right through it.

"She's fine," I said in answer to her question. "The kids are fine, too."

"That's good," she said. It was hard to know if she really meant it.

Mary Lou has nice eyes, and a more than pretty face. It's a long face, which goes well with her tall, statuesque appearance. She's a truly beautiful woman, but one with more cunning than a fox in a hen house. She is convinced that our break-up was the result of my desire for much younger women. Mary Lou is in her mid-thirties.

Mary Lou is, perhaps, right about my affinity for younger women being the cause of our demise as a couple. However, it was probably more my desire for numbers rather than youth that tolled the death knell for our relationship.

I couldn't help but remember that the guy who called himself Jesus had more or less made that observation. And I still like Mary Lou a lot, maybe more than any other woman I've ever known.

"So, how are you doing, Mary Lou? How's the job going?" Mary Lou works in the public relations department for a major corporation, one whose products are totally unnecessary. There are a lot of corporations like that, all of which put tremendous stress on public relations.

"It's a job," she said. "It pays the mortgage and my car payments."

I already knew she didn't like the job, that she merely tolerated it. She works with a lot of incompetent bozos who spent all their time kissing the chairman of the board's rear end. They are well-rewarded for this degrading act, which bothers

Mary Lou a great deal. She is a very intelligent woman.

"I was hoping you'd have found something else by now," I sympathized.

"Public relations jobs aren't easy to find," she said, "especially those that will pay a woman a living wage."

"I guess not."

"Let's talk about something more pleasant than my job," she suggested. "For example, when are you going to take me on a cruise?"

"I didn't know I was," I replied, knowing she was getting ready to do a little teasing.

"I don't guess you remember, do you?"

"You're going to tell me I promised to take you on a cruise."

"You're right. Would you like me to list all the other things you promised me?" She liked to make fun of what she called my convenient memory. Frankly, I don't think my memory's all that bad. And I don't think I've promised women as much as they attribute to me.

"Well, according to what you've told me in the past, I don't think I have time to hear all the promises I allegedly made to you. I have to go to work this afternoon."

She laughed. "You're right. I will need about a week to list them all."

Mary Lou likes a good joke as much as the next

person, but I didn't think she was in on the Jesus charade. Still, since she knows some of my friends, I thought she might know the identity of the perpetrator.

"Have you seen any of my pals recently?" I asked.

"I saw Jimmy Joe a week ago. He bought me a drink at Friday's." The reference was to Jimmy Joe Johnson, a cowboy booted compadre who sells oil deals. He's never been able to sell me one, but I never have any money. He sells enough to drive a new Cadillac and wear fashionable western-style suits. He wears a big white cowboy hat on a balding dome, but a lot of folks to whom he's sold oil deals think a black hat would be more appropriate. Jimmy Joe may not be entirely honest. But he's also not the kind of guy to mock God. For one thing, I don't think he knows who God is, even though at one time he gave serious thought to being a minister. Perhaps *serious* is too strong a word for one of Jimmy Joe's thoughts.

"How's ol' Jimmy Joe doing? I haven't seen him in three or four weeks."

"You can count your blessings," Mary Lou said. "The man's more than a tad off-center."

"I don't know why you say things like that about Jimmy Joe. He always speaks very highly of you."

"He should," she said. "I'm certainly the classiest woman he's ever been around, and I think that includes his mother."

"That's a really low blow, even for you, Mary Lou."

She shrugged her shoulders. "It's the truth. You ought to have seen the slut he was with the afternoon he bought me a drink. If he didn't pick her up off Harry Hines Boulevard, I'm a nigger aviator."

Mary Lou is a bit of a racist, though she claims to be pale in comparison to me. Harry Hines is a Dallas street that has a reputation for hookers and porno shops.

"Jimmy Joe's choice of women friends isn't the best," I agreed, "but he's not one to think in terms of a meaningful relationship."

"He's not one to think, period," she grumbled. "The good whores turn him down."

I laughed. Mary Lou has never been a Jimmy Joe Johnson fan, not from the first minute in which I introduced them. She has always considered Jimmy Joe a conniving rascal, one who would rather make one dollar dishonestly than ten dollars honestly. As for me, I can't help but like ol' Jimmy Joe. He's what he is. More importantly, we were in college together, which was when he was a ministerial student. Jimmy Joe flunked out the first year and renounced the faith. He had prayed to God for help in getting through freshman English, but God didn't help him.

Of course, Jimmy Joe didn't get any help from God in any of his classes. He flunked them all. Jimmy Joe had counted on God doing his studying for him while he played dominos. God obviously had no interest in the subject matter, so Jimmy Joe figured it was a sign that he wasn't to be a minister.

I didn't argue with Jimmy Joe's logic back then, and I don't argue with it now. Arguing with Jimmy Joe is like debating a turnip. If deep thought was like water, Jimmy Joe would never get his feet wet.

Mary Lou and I had our breakfast and talked until about eight forty-five. I grilled her and she grilled me, but the end result was that I became convinced she knew nothing about the man calling himself Jesus.

I have to admit, the entire scenerio was making me a bit shaky. My nerves felt like a ball of worms all tangled up and wiggling to get free. It would be just my luck not to know the real Jesus when he returned to earth.

III

Billy Bob Raintree isn't one of Dallas' premier lawyers. To the contrary, Billy Bob is to the legal profession what a shade tree mechanic is to the automotive industry. Those of us who know him well often wonder how he managed to escape with a degree from Baylor Law School. But Billy Bob is one of those good ol' boys who acts a lot simpler than he really is.

When he was an undergraduate at Baylor, Billy Bob once stole a baby camel from a circus that came to town. He put the camel in an elevator in the Armstrong-Browning Library and took it to the floor that houses the Elizabeth Barrett Browning Collection. The room contains such worthwhile memorabilia as one of Elizabeth's handkerchiefs and so on. Such relics are alleged to be inspirational.

A man once told me that if he gave a billion dollars to a university, he could the following year ask where the money went and no one would have a clue. He said giving money to a university is like pouring it down a well. The Armstrong-Browning Library is testimony to the man's views.

Of course, Billy Bob didn't have anything against the Armstrong-Browning Library. He just figured it was a good place to keep a camel. Just like he thought a particular English professor's office was the best place to leave a boa constrictor, or that a particular math professor's desk drawer was the best place to leave dog dung.

But Billy Bob didn't relegate all his time in college to dealing with camels, snakes and dogs. Practically every night during his undergraduate and law school years, Billy Bob went on one-man panty raids. And not one time during all those years did any girl, even one of the real bow wows, throw him a pair of panties. The girls would all look out their dorm windows and echo a common refrain, "It's just Billy Bob." In spite of his dogged determination, he was of all men most ignored. He tried to get a listing in *The Guinness World Book of Records* for unsuccessful panty raids, but instead got a rejection letter from one of the editors.

In spite of Billy Bob's ineptness, he made a decent living as an attorney, primarily handling divorce cases. After he had made somewhat of a reputation for himself, none of his cases ever went to trial. Other lawyers can't stand to be in the courtroom with him, nor can judges, because his inane questioning over minute points gives everyone the screaming meemies.

Billy Bob doesn't bother me that much, because when I am around him I disassociate myself from my surroundings. It is the only way to avoid embarrassment.

It was because of the man who called himself Jesus that I called Billy Bob and invited him to lunch. I figured Billy Bob might have had a part in sending him my way. And just to make the lunch a little more interesting, I also called my house and invited the man who called himself Jesus to join us. When the man asked about transportation, I told him to take a DART bus, or have whoever hired him to pick him up. Or better still, to just transport himself supernaturally.

He laughed, said he'd take a DART bus. I figured if he could find a DART bus driver awake at ten-thirty or eleven o'clock in the morning, that would be supernatural enough for me. When his eyes weren't looking at me, it was easier to be tacky.

Our luncheon was scheduled for eleven forty-five at Raphael's Restaurant on McKinney, where the cuisine is obviously Mexican. It was my choice because Billy Bob likes Mexican food and I like margaritas. I have often considered opening a Mexican restaurant, because where else can you make such a profit on refried beans, rice and ground beef. Except for nachos, it is difficult to have any respect for Mexican food.

Anyway, the man who called himself Jesus was already at the restaurant when I arrived. He was wearing a nondescript off-the-rack sports coat, slacks that didn't go too well with it, and what looked like a pair of old Hush Puppy shoes. He had on a button-down collar white shirt and no tie, and his hair was mussed from what I guessed was the cold north wind that was battering the area. I didn't bother to offer him my comb.

We were shown to a table and asked if we wanted a drink. I chose a margarita and the man who called himself Jesus asked for water.

"What have you been doing this morning?" I asked.

"I've been cleaning the house," he said. "It was a real mess."

I shrugged my shoulders. "I usually have a maid service come in once a week."

"They obviously don't do windows, clean behind the furniture or scrub the kitchen floor," he said.

"I've always thought they did a good job," I said, "but I don't check everything that thoroughly."

The way he talked about housework, you'd have thought it was the most important thing in the world. And, of course, that made those doing it seem just as important. He didn't have to convince me. I've always thought the most important work a woman can do is housework. Unfortunately, a lot of women don't share my enthusiasm for their importance.

The waiter brought my margarita, the man's water.

"What have you been doing today?" the man asked.

"Well, I almost caused an editor to have a heart attack by getting to work so early."

"Did you enjoy your breakfast with Ms. Magruder?"

"How did you . . ."

Billy Bob interrupted. "Hey, guys, I'm not late am I?"

Questioning the man on how he knew about my breakfast date with Mary Lou would have to wait. Billy Bob had appeared, seemingly on cue, and he was dressed as dapper as ever. He was wearing an odd color designer suit, with a stranger than fiction tie and blue Nike running shoes. Billy Bob gave up regular shoes several years ago, now wears nothing but running shoes. He doesn't, however, run or jog. He thinks such shoes make a fashion statement. I read somewhere that athletic shoe sales in America annually average out to eight pair per person. Billy Bob buys his share, but I haven't been keeping up with the trend. Somewhere, someone is wearing shoes I should have bought.

"Sit down, Billy Bob," I said. "I believe you know J.C., don't you?"

"No, can't say as I do," he replied, taking the extended hand of the man who called himself Jesus.

"My name is Jesus," the man said.

"Oh, for crying out loud," I said. "Why don't you guys can the crap and the sacrilege?"

"Billy Bob took on a quizzical look. "Jesus? You mean like in Jesus Christ?"

"I am Jesus Christ," the man said.

I glanced furtively around, hoping no one was listening to our conversation."

"Did you hear that, Mark?" Billy Bob asked a bit too loudly. "This man is Jesus Christ. You've outdone yourself this time, Mark. I can't believe I'm having lunch with Jesus Christ."

"Tone it down a bit," I growled, "You know damn well who this guy is, Billy Bob. My guess is that he's on your payroll."

"Whoa!" Billy Bob said. "What's this all about?"

"You know."

"No, I don't know."

You can look Billy Bob square in the eyes, and you still can't tell whether or not he's lying or telling the truth. You never could, even before he became a lawyer. Of course, his ability to lie with a straight face has been a great asset in his profession.

The man laughed. "He really has no idea as to what you're talking about, Mark."

I snorted. "He's the kind of guy who would pull a trick like this."

The man sighed. "I keep telling you it's no trick. I am Jesus Christ, the Son of God."

Billy Bob gave the man an incredulous look. "You're serious, aren't you?"

The man just smiled.

Billy Bob stuttered, "Hey, Mark, I . . . well, never mind."

If Billy Bob was putting on an act of surprise, it was a good one. And I know he's capable of doing a better job of acting than some of those Hollywood people who get paid to do it. But I was beginning to believe he really didn't know anything about the man who called himself Jesus. Of course, when it came to acting, I was beginning to believe the man who called himself Jesus was in a class all by himself. He was good. Damn good.

The man looked bemused by the entire scenerio, but before I could level any additional accusations the waiter came to take our order. Since all Mexican food except nachos tastes the same to me, I just told the waiter to bring me another margarita and something without onions or tomatoes. My companions ordered big Mexican dinners with all the trimmings. The man asked for another glass of water, and Billy Bob ordered a Mexican beer.

I noticed Billy Bob looked a little green around the gills, but didn't think much of it since he often looks that way. He kept glancing at the man, then quickly looking away, as though he was extremely nervous.

I addressed a question to the man who called himself Jesus. "Lawyers don't have much of a shot at Heaven, do they?"

"The Kingdom isn't denied to specific professions," he replied. "Only the individual can deny Heaven for himself, and that only because of what is in his heart. God's Laws and man's laws can't be equated on the same basis."

"I don't believe you answered my question."

"I answered, you just weren't interested in hear-ing," he said. "Lawyers, doctors, janitors, report-ers . . . none have a shot at Heaven without accept-ance of God's Way. And any man exposed to God's Word is capable of judging himself."

Billy Bob squirmed in his chair, then meekly said, "That's right, Mark. You need to quit trying to put me down in front of Jesus."

I gave him an incredulous look. "What?"

"You heard me," he said. "I'm sure no saint, that's true. But there's no point in you trying to belittle me in front of Jesus."

I laughed. "That does it. Now I know you're in on this deal, Billy Bob."

"I don't know what deal you're talking about, but I'm not in on anything."

"Billy Bob really doesn't have any idea as to what you're talking about," the man who called himself Jesus reiterated. "I told you that some of your friends would accept who I am before you did, and you now have evidence of that in Billy Bob."

"You have to be kidding," I said, chuckling. "This is the Billy Bob Raintree who in college set a bridge on fire, who stole a bulldozer and ran it into a creek, who put a camel in the Armstrong-Browning Library, who unsuccessfully tried to make out with every girl on campus. And now you tell me he's going to just make like a sheep and accept some clown who claims to be Jesus."

"You underestimate a lot of things, Mark, not the least of which is God's grace and power."

"C'mon, enough's enough. Drop the Jesus act, tell me who you really are and let's all have a good laugh. It has been a well-played joke, and I'll admit to even having a couple of doubts."

"I still don't know what you're talking about," Billy Bob said, "but this man is the Son of God."

Billy Bob was so serious looking that I couldn't help but laugh. "You've outdone yourself on this one, Billy Bob. But like I said, enough's enough. Can the act."

The man who called himself Jesus looked at me somberly and said, "I'm not acting." The sincerity with which he spoke caused a tingle to run down my spine. There were maybe even a few goose bumps. You know, the kind you get when you hear the Star Spangled Banner at a ball game.

Fortunately, the waiter arrived with our food. I ordered another margarita, shook my head in mock dismay, and again told Billy Bob and the man who called himself Jesus to get serious.

Then the man started talking to Billy Bob, mostly about spiritual things as I recall. And I don't believe I had ever seen Billy Bob listen so intently to anyone. Up until then, I had figured Billy Bob's attention span to be about five seconds maximum. But he was listening to this guy, nodding his head and agreeing with everything he said. That's another thing that puzzled me. I'd never known Billy Bob to agree with anyone. In an political argument, if you took the Republican side you could count on Billy Bob to take the Democrat position. And if you chose the Democrat position, he would take the Republican view.

Billy Bob loves to argue.

As to all the spiritual stuff the guy told him . . . well, I can't remember it. And I can't be faulted for that because even the disciples didn't remember everything Jesus said and did. If they did, they didn't write it all down for us to read. It's a good thing, too, since most folks have a tough enough time reading what little there is of the Gospels in the New Testament.

I think of the Gospels in the New Testament as being kind of a *Readers Digest* condensed version of Jesus' life and work on earth.

Anyway, I'd invited an old friend, looney tunes as he was, to lunch to find out if he was in on the Jesus gag and, after we had eaten and talked, he became a real disciple of this cat who was going around calling himself Jesus.

It looked to me like the joke was on Billy Bob, not me.

IV

After determining in my own mind that Billy Bob Raintree was not responsible for the man who called himself Jesus, I became somewhat irritated that my attorney friend had fallen under the man's spell. I was not angry at the man, but rather at Billy Bob for his obvious naivete. It was not like him to be so easily duped. To the contrary, I expected him to do the duping.

The man's knowledge of the New Testament, the whole Bible for that matter, was incredible. Or, at least, it seemed incredible to me. He was able to make plausible what I considered to be contradictions in the Bible. And he did it all with a common sense approach that made me wonder why I hadn't previously been able to comprehend what the Bible was saying.

Still, I was not ready to believe he was anything other than a charlatan, an unbelievably good actor who had been employed to toy with my mind. I had to admit he was doing a good job.

However, I couldn't even explain my own actions and attitudes regarding the man who called himself Jesus. To invite him to be a permanent house guest, after having known him for less than twenty-four hours, was not like me. I like my privacy, a fact to which my ex-wife will attest. But around this man, I found myself reacting and saying things I considered totally contrary to my normal behavior.

Forgive me for belaboring a point, but it also bothered me that Billy Bob saw something in the man that I couldn't see. It's not that I consider Billy Bob a bad person, but he's certainly no spiritual giant, either. As candidates for Heaven, I would consider myself a couple of notches above him.

What I couldn't get out of my mind was what Billy Bob said to me after lunch. The man who called himself Jesus had already left at the time, I presumed to catch a DART bus back to the vicinity of my house. "Can't you see it, Mark?" Billy Bob had said. "That man really is the Son of God."

"You're as full of crap as a Christmas turkey," I replied. "If you're in on this gag, I'll nail your ass if it's the last thing I ever do."

But Billy Bob was as serious as lip cancer when he said, "I can't believe you're so blind."

Though Billy Bob is as hard to read as the small print on an eye chart at an optometrist's office, I was beginning to believe he wasn't putting me on, that he really believed what he said.

So, during the afternoon while I was trying to write a couple of stories for the morning edition, I was wondering how this man who called himself Jesus could exercise so much power in so short a time. I was willing to admit that he had exercised some sort of power on me, but thought he'd put an even bigger clamp on Billy Bob.

It was as hard to figure as how the State of Texas could cut millions of dollars out of its budget, unless a lot of unnecessary stuff was being budgeted for anyway. Surely the politicians wouldn't do something like that.

I completed my assignments about mid-afternoon and decided to see if my best friend at the paper, Bobo Harrison, wanted a cup of coffee. Bobo's a sports writer, not by choice but because he can only write in cliches. He speaks good cliche, too, but can usually be counted on to be supportive of my ideas about DART, local, state and national government. Bobo draws the line on agreeing with me about world affairs, but that doesn't bother me since he thinks Philadelphia is another country.

Bobo is maybe six-feet six-inches tall and weighs in at about two-hundred sixty pounds. His college days were spent playing defensive tackle for University of Texas-El Paso, drinking beer and visiting Boys Town just across the border in Juarez. Bobo hasn't changed all that much in twenty-five years, except that he now writes about football instead of playing it. He still drinks a lot of beer and would be visiting Boys Town if it wasn't a career's trip from Dallas. El Paso is more than six hundred miles to the west.

For those unfamiliar with Boys Town, it's the equivalent of an entire city of brothels.

Bobo's married and has a couple of kids. He takes the kids seriously, but not the marriage. He is always looking for a new woman, but normally settles for another beer. Cocktail waitresses familiar with his drinking habits usually serve him two or three beers at a time. By the time I can guzzle a margarita, Bobo can put away a half dozen beers.

"Hell yes, I'd like a cup of coffee," Bobo said, swinging his feet off his desk and onto the floor. "You buying?"

"Yeah, I'm buying. I'll even buy you a pack of Twinkies if you like."

He chuckled, patted his belly and said, "I'd better lay off the sweets. I need to lose a few pounds. Been on a diet for about a week now."

As we started walking toward the newspaper's canteen, I asked, "This diet you're on, have you quit drinking beer?"

He gave me an incredulous look and said, "It's not that strict a diet. I'm just trying to eat a lot of fish now, stuff like that."

"Ugh, I don't like fish."

"I like 'em."

"Well, I was going to invite you over to Joe Miller's for a few brews after work, but I don't want to screw up your diet." Joe Miller's is a bar where a lot of journalism types hang out.

"I'm not one to turn down a brew," Bobo said, "What time are you talking about?"

"About five-fifteen."

"I'll have tomorrow's column done by then."

"What are you writing about?"

"Hell, I don't know."

We got our coffee, which looked a few days old, and found a table. The place was pretty empty.

"I see where your competition, Hop Gulfless, is still crying about the Cowboys salary structure," I said. "He'd make a helluva lot better players agent than a sports writer."

Gulfless, who I thought wrote sports like a freshman in high school, had once worked for our paper. But the competition offered him more money so he skipped to their side. His defection came after our paper spent hundreds of thousands of dollars promoting him, piling hype higher than a Mount Everest of raw sewage. Hop never thought any of the Dallas Cowboys players were making enough money, that they were being brutalized by the team's ownership. It seemed that he wrote about it constantly.

I figured ol' Hop for more than stupid. I figured him for a Communist. Of course, he has the same agent used by some players.

Bobo shrugged his shoulders. "Anything I say about Hop sounds like sour grapes, but the stupid bastard thinks a two hundred hitter ought to be making a million a year. I have to think he's queer for jocks."

"One of the reasons I want you to have a few beers with me is because I want to introduce you to a guy. He claims to be Jesus Christ."

Bobo gave me a disbelieving look, then chuckled. "You're putting me on."

I should say here that I didn't suspect Bobo of being the one who sent the man who called himself Jesus into my life. Bobo likes to hear a good joke, and he tries to tell one occasionally. But he rarely remembers the punch line of a joke, and he's never been one for pranks. Bobo is more likely to be the butt of a joke than to play one, and since he is often unaware when a joke is being played on him, most of his friends don't even bother. Bobo's the kind of guy who takes on a puzzled look when he hears a joke on Monday, then breaks out laughing when he finally understands it on Tuesday or Wednesday. If the joke lingers in his mind more than two days, he won't catch on because he will forget it.

Now don't get the idea Bobo is dense or anything like that. He's not what you'd call a deep thinker, but being a sports writer doesn't require the mind of a Plato.

I told Bobo all that occurred since the previous evening, including breakfast with Mary Lou and lunch with Billy Bob.

He grinned. "It's that damn Mary Lou. You know how she likes a practical joke. She's one fine looking woman, too. I don't know why you're not more interested in her." Then he turned somber and said, "Of course, it could be that little asshole Billy Bob."

Bobo is not one of Billy Bob's fans, the main reason being that in one of our Sunday touch football games, Billy Bob used his head to butt Bobo in the crotch. It was the only time I've ever seen Bobo cry. It was my pleading and Billy Bob's speed that saved him from certain death at Bobo's hands.

"For some reason, I don't think it's Billy Bob," I said. "I may be wrong, but I really don't think he knew the man until lunch today."

Bobo snarled, "He's a devious, shifty little bastard."

"Well, he is a lawyer."

"Enough said."

"That reminds me of a new lawyer joke I just heard."

"Let's hear it," Bobo said.

"Did you know that scientists are now using lawyers instead of white mice for their experiments?"

"No, I didn't know," Bobo replied, seriously.

"There are three reasons, the first being that there is a shortage of white mice."

Bobo gave me a blank look.

I continued, "The second reason is that scientists don't get attached to lawyers like they do to white mice, and the third reason is that there are certain things white mice won't do."

When Bobo realized I had finished the joke, he chuckled. It was obvious, however, that he didn't understand the joke. It didn't surprise me. Maybe he would catch it tomorrow.

We had refills on coffee, then went back to our respective desks to finish out the day. I telephoned the man who called himself Jesus and asked him to meet us at Joe Miller's. As an afterthought, I called Jimmy Joe Johnson and asked him to also meet us.

Joe Miller's is kind of dark, kind of noisy. But there's a table in the back of the place that I particularly like. From it you can see all that's going on in the place. That's where I usually sit, with my back to the wall. I got to the bar a little earlier than the after-five crowd normally arrives so I could commandeer the table. The man who called himself Jesus was already sitting at it.

He greeted me with, "I figured this was where you'd want to sit."

The guy was getting a little spooky, but I simply said, "Yeah, this table will be fine."

He was dressed just as he had been at lunch, which was no surprise. In the brief time I'd known him, from a fashion standpoint he hadn't shown me too much in terms of style. We chatted for a while, about nothing I can remember, and then Jimmy Joe arrived.

"Jimmy Joe," I said, "I'd like you to meet J.C. Smith."

As they were shaking hands, the man said, "My name is Jesus."

Jimmy Joe didn't say anything for a few seconds, then responded, "That name's familiar."

Now even though Jimmy Joe had been a ministerial student, he'd been away from the faith for a long time. And because I know how his mind works, I wasn't surprised by his statement. I knew he was sizing the man who called himself Jesus up as a potential prospect for an oil deal.

Jimmy Joe continued, "You're not from Amarillo, are you? I think maybe I knew a Jesus family out around Amarillo. Or was it around Lubbock?"

The man laughed. "We've never met. I can assure you that you don't know me."

Jimmy Joe turned his attention on me. "How's it going, Hoss? Been a while, been a while. What are you drinking there?"

I was nursing a margarita, the man had a glass of water. I told Jimmy Joe what I had and he said, "Got to have a bourbon myself. Maybe I'll have burbon and Dr. Pepper."

I grimaced at the thought of his selection, but Jimmy Joe isn't bound by the same tastes as most mortals. The waitress wasn't startled by his order, but in Joe Miller's waitresses aren't startled by much of anything. A lot of Jimmy Joes hang out at Joe Miller's.

Turning his attention to the man, Jimmy Joe asked, "What line of work are you in, Jesus? Do you want me to call you Jesus or J.C.?"

The man smiled and said, "Whatever's most comfortable to you."

"J.C.'s more comfortable for me," I said.

"Hell, what's your comfort got to do with anything?" Jimmy Joe asked.

"Maybe you should just call me J.C.," the man said.

"No, by god, I'll call you Jesus. Mark needs to lighten up on ordering everyone around. What line of work are you in?"

"My principal work is being man's savior," he replied.

I groaned. "Please, let it lie."

"You're shitin' me," Jimmy Joe said to the man who called himself Jesus. "Is it pretty profitable?"

"It depends on what you call profit," the man answered.

"Now I remember," Jimmy Joe said, excitedly. "There's a Jesus in the Bible. You're that Jesus, aren't you?"

"Hey, this is ridiculous," I said. "How much did you pay this guy to pull this prank on me, Jimmy Joe?"

Jimmy Joe looked blank, which is not an unusual look for him. "What are you talking about?" he asked.

"You know damn well what I'm talking about. You hired this guy to give me a hard time."

"I ain't hired nobody," Jimmy Joe said. "And if I was you, Mark, I'd be a little careful about what I said. With Jesus right here with us, you ought to be scared shitless."

"This guy's not Jesus," I said. "At least, he's not the Jesus in the New Testament."

"Hey, I'm not taking any chances. I'm going to drink this Dr. Pepper, but I'm passing on the bourbon."

"Unbelievable," I said.

Fortunately, Bobo entered the place about that time. When his eyes grew accustomed to the dark, he saw me waving at him. En route to the table he intercepted the waitress and ordered three beers.

I introduced Bobo to the man who called himself Jesus. He already knew Jimmy Joe, had even borrowed money to buy into one of Jimmy Joe's oil deals.

"How's our oil well doing?" Bobo asked Jimmy Joe.

"It's coming right along, Hoss. I expect we'll be hearing something any day now."

"We'd better, or I'm going to shove one of your cowboy boots up your ass," Bobo threatened.

Jimmy Joe gave an uneasy laugh. "A little patience, Bobo. These things don't happen overnight." Jimmy Joe is a couple of inches shorter than Bobo and a lot leaner, but with his cowboy boots on he looks just as tall.

Bobo started sucking on a beer and then asked the man, "You interested in football?"

"Of course, he's interested in football," Jimmy Joe answered. "Mark introduced this gentleman as J.C. Smith, but he's really Jesus. You know, the one in the Bible."

Bobo grunted. "Mark told me. But I didn't ask you, asshole. I asked Jesus if he was interested in football."

"It's okay," the man replied. "I don't have much tolerance for highly paid, free-living and sniveling athletes, but there's nothing wrong with the game."

"Well, hallelujah," Bobo said. "It's good to know someone else doesn't appreciate the seven figure salaries being paid to a bunch of cry baby jocks."

"I sort of thought you might like my answer," the man said, showing a bemused look. "I know it's how Mark feels."

"Everyone knows how I feel," I grumbled. "But can you honestly sit there and tell me Jimmy Joe didn't put you up to approaching me last night?"

"I can," he replied, "because no one put me up to approaching you."

Bobo asked, "What do you think about the Cowboys and Eagles on Sunday?"

"I don't really think about it," the man said.

"Well, you being Jesus and all, you ought to be able to give us an idea about who's going to win," Bobo said. "If you were going to bet, who would you bet on?"

"What you need to understand, Bobo," the man said, "is that God in his infinite wisdom and knowledge knows who is going to win the game, but doesn't care. God doesn't determine the outcome of the game, of any game for that matter."

"If God doesn't determine the winner, who does?" Bobo asked.

"The choices made by the coaches and players, their particular skills, that determines who wins."

"God does kind of favor the Cowboys, doesn't He?" Jimmy Joe asked, grinning.

The man shook his head in resignation. "If every Cowboys player was a Christian and every Eagles player was an atheist, God still wouldn't give the Cowboys a victory. God gives every man the right of choice, and his choices determine the way things happen. Jimmy Joe, what you and Bobo are trying to do is trivialize God. You want God to be concerned about something as trivial as a football game."

Bobo grumbled. "I thought maybe God would go with Coach Landry because he's a good Christian.

"He's not a Christian in order to win football games," the man said. "He's a Christian because he made a choice, a personal commitment."

"If being a Christian's not going to help you in life, what's the point?" I asked.

"If winning or losing a football game is all there is to life, Mark, then I'd have to think that life isn't worth living," the man said. "Winning in anything isn't all there is to life. Being a Christian helps you endure losing, and it should make you more humble and appreciative when you're victorious."

"You have an answer for everything, don't you?"

"God has an answer," he said, "but it's not going

to always be to your satisfaction."

"What you say makes a lot of sense," Bobo chimed in. "When I was playing college ball, we used to pray before every game, but we didn't win many."

"What coaches and football teams call prayer falls far short of what prayer really is," the man said. "Prayer should be meaningful, not a formality, and not a request for something as trivial as victory in a football game. And it certainly shouldn't be for show."

"Well, I figured you were honoring God when you prayed," Jimmy Joe said.

"You don't honor God with prayer," the man said. "You honor yourself. You make yourself better than beasts because you've made a choice for the best. But if you pray, pray for something worthwhile, not for the jocks you like to be better than the jocks someone else likes."

I laughed. "You'll have Jimmy Joe praying for some of his oil wells to come in."

The man smiled. "That's not something you need to pray for. You just need to drill in the right spot."

"What if I pray that we'll drill in the right spot?" Jimmy Joe asked.

"I hope you won't do that, Jimmy Joe," the man said. "I hope you won't give God credit for having you drill in the right spot, because then you'll be blaming Him when you don't drill in the right spot.

Hiring a good geologist is a much better bet than a selfish prayer."

"What are we supposed to pray for then," I asked, "just that God's Will be done."

The man looked at me with those piercing eyes and said, "Any man who knows and follows me knows God's Will."

I argued, "According to you, if we were in a war with the Russians, God wouldn't be on either side."

"I didn't say that," the man said, "but God would not fight the battles for this country. The war would be man's choosing, whether Russian or American, and the victor would be the country with the superior technology and the proper use of it."

"Then calling on God for help is a waste of time," I said.

The man looked at me with resignation and replied, "Has it ever occurred to you that persons who believe in God often use their mental capabilities to a far greater extent that those who don't? Has it ever occurred to you that a country where Christianity is freely practiced is normally a country where a man's mind is not handicapped, where because of choice he can reach inside himself for answers and solutions to the most perplexing problems in life?"

As previously stated, the man was deep. I think I understand what he was saying, that because of freedom of choice a country that espouses Christianity has more going for it technologically than one that doesn't. The reason being, of course, is that freedom encourages thought. The country that forces a particular ideology down the throats of its citizens can't expect much in the way of creative thought from its people.

"What you're saying is that while God may not fight a battle for you, the very fact that you believe in and trust God might decide the battle in your favor," I concluded.

"Belief in what is right is a strong motivator," the man said. "And belief in God has many times enabled the weak to often overcome the strong."

We ordered another round of drinks. The man who called himself Jesus got another glass of water. Persons who I didn't even know had now crowded around our table. They were listening intently to everything the man said. Even though I didn't know the people, it was embarrassing to me. It didn't seem to bother Bobo and Jimmy Joe at all.

"You say that God is just," I said. "How does the destruction of all those Jews during World War Two fit into this justness that you talk about?" I asked.

His eyes showed great sadness as he responded. "I have already told you that God has given all men the right to choose good or evil. It is the choice of the individual man. Obviously, Adolph Hitler chose evil, and many chose to follow his example of evil."

"Was Hitler the anti-Christ?" someone asked.

The man who called himself Jesus replied, "There have been many anti-Christs. There are many in today's world, and there will be many in the future."

I figured it was his way of saying Hitler wasn't the only one operating during his particular era.

"Maybe all those Jews were killed because their forefathers rejected Christ," someone said.

The man who called himself Jesus shook his head in resignation. "They died because all men have the right of choice, and because some men chose evil instead of good. Those same men are responsible for the deaths of many more persons who claimed to be Christians. The evil for which Hitler was responsible was not confined to the Jews."

"How do you think God will judge Hitler?" someone asked. "What sort of punishment will he receive?"

The man who called himself Jesus took a sip of water, paused momentarily before answering, "God does not have to judge Hitler or any like him. He judged himself, just as each of you will judge yourselves."

"What do you mean, judge ourselves?" I asked.

"You have access to the truth, to The Way," he said. "It is your decision whether to accept The Way or not. In so doing, you judge yourself."

I argued, "There are a lot of things in the Bible that I just can't justify."

"It isn't your place to justify God's method and means of salvation," he said. "You have only the right to choose whether to accept it or not."

The conversation continued for two or three hours, maybe even more. I'm not sure how many margaritas I consumed, nor how many beers Bobo stowed away in the reservoir he calls a stomach. I also can't recall much of the dialogue that took place, only remember that a lot of really heavy religious stuff came from the mouth of the man who called himself Jesus. What I can tell you is that my mind was in a whirl, like a windmill that couldn't decide on the direction to turn.

Bobo finally broke the mood of the participants in the conversation when he said, "I'd still like to know how the game's going to come out Sunday."

Almost everyone laughed, including the man who called himself Jesus. Jimmy Joe didn't laugh. He was tightlipped and serious, more serious than I'd ever seen him before. That worried me, along with the fact that everyone other than me seemed to be accepting this man who called himself Jesus as the real thing.

V

Joe Don Barnes joined the police department right after graduation from Howard Payne University, which is a small Baptist school located at Brownwood, Texas. Brownwood is a two or three hour drive southwest of Fort Worth, depending on the speed at which you want to drive. It may seem a little ridiculous and obvious to say that driving time depends on the speed at which you drive, but being redundant and obvious sort of symbolizes the way things are in the Brownwood area. This is not to say that Joe Don is redundant or obvious in his speech, only that he spent a couple of years at Brownwood.

Actually, Joe Don is a city boy, if you want to categorize Dallas as a city. Some people just classify it as a place where Texas farm and ranch kids go after they grow up and graduate from high school or college. Illegal aliens from Mexico, Detroit and New York come to Dallas to allegedly work. However, it's hard to catch them doing any.

Anyway, Joe Don was born in these environs, grew up in them and then moved to the country. And when I say country, I'm not referring to Brownwood, though the area can probably be classified as such. Joe Don, however, took a much more drastic step, initially moving to Fayetteville, Arkansas.

The person who thinks Brownwood is country needs to spend a little time in Fayetteville, where the only culture you'll find is in a churn full of buttermilk gone bad.

As to why Joe Don ended up in an area where people sing out *Soohey Pig* with the same reverence as *Amazing Grace,* he was recruited to play football for the University of Arkansas Razorbacks. The man who recruited him, and who was the coach, has since become an unemployed network television college football commentator, one who often spouted off about the importance of education to student athletes, the integrity of college football, the pureness of University of Arkansas athletes, and so on.

This is the same guy who, when Joe Don got pissed, bolted the team and came home to mama, gave him two thousand in cash to return to Fayetteville. I figured Joe Don sold out cheap when you consider that he was being asked to return to Fayetteville. This former coach is a real *holier-than-thou,* and while he may be able to spell integrity, he never practiced it.

Joe Don finally got tired of the coach's sermonizing without substance, used what was left of his two thousand along with a good chunk of laundry money, and transferred to Howard Payne. He didn't go to Brownwood for religious reasons, but simply because it was a place where he could play a little football, ride in a few rodeos, and get his degree.

That's right, Joe Don liked playing cowboy, so he did a little bull riding. He was pretty good, too, even thought about rodeoing professionally, but was never able to keep a pinch between his cheek and gum. The fact that he kept swallowing his snuff caused him to realize it wasn't God's Will for him to be a rodeo cowboy.

Even though Joe Don was quick to give God credit for his demise in the rodeo arena, if any Baptist religious training was instilled in him, I've never seen it. Oh, I'm sure he believes in God, probably has since he was a child, but that belief has never altered him doing anything he wanted to do, which resulted in some severe marital problems. Like me, Joe Don is divorced.

Joe Don is a little over six feet tall and weighs in at slightly more than two hundred pounds. He's square-jawed, has brown eyes, and his hair is cut short. He looks like a police detective is supposed to look.

About the only other thing I can add is that Joe Don hasn't heeded the advice of the U.S. Surgeon General. He exhales more smoke than a dying diesel automobile. Despite this obvious character flaw (in my opinion cigarettes rank on the list with tomatoes and onions), Joe Don and I have maintained a strong friendship over the years.

There are advantages to having a friend who is a

police captain, not the least of which is access to certain information not available to ordinary citizens. Because Joe Don has access to computerized information on the criminal element and others, I asked him to run a check on the man who called himself Jesus.

"I don't think we're going to have too much luck chasing a *Jesus* alias," Joe Don told me.

"Probably not," I said, "which is why I brought you a glass with the man's fingerprints on it."

He grinned. "Damn, you're really out to get this guy, aren't you?"

"Not really. The person I'm really out to get is the one who hired him for this charade."

"With all the information sources you have at the paper, I'd think you'd be able to get a line on him there."

I sighed. "I've tried, believe me. But I've gotten nowhere."

"Has it ever occurred to you that the taxpayers might not appreciate me checking stuff out for you at their expense?"

"Damn it, Joe Don, are you going to check for me or not?"

"Don't get your ass in an uproar," he chided. "I'm going to take care of you, pal. It'll take a while though. Do you want to buy me a little lunch?"

I complained, "You don't know the meaning of a little lunch."

Joe Don used a police car with flashing lights

and siren to transport us to the Highland Park Cafeteria on Knox, which is one of my favorite places to eat. In fact, some national magazines have rated Highland Park Cafeteria as one of the best places to eat in Dallas. The only weakness the place has is that it doesn't have margaritas or any other type booze on the menu.

Since I was buying, Joe Don decided we'd bypass standing in line and help ourselves to the upstairs buffet. "It's not cheap," Joe Don said, "but you can get the paper to pick up the tab. Just tell your editor that you're working on a big story and had to entertain a source."

"I couldn't do that," I said. "It wouldn't be the truth."

Joe Don rolled his eyes, then loaded a plate with beef brisket, smothered steak and fried chicken."

"Are you going to eat any vegetables?" I asked.

"I'm going to put those on another plate."

The buffet is a pitch until you win deal, meaning you can eat all you want or until you can't even waddle out of the place.

I said, "You can come back for seconds or thirds, you know."

Undaunted, he said, "I intend to."

By the time Joe Don got a plate full of vegetables, another plate full of various salads and fruits, and a platter of bread, our table looked like the picture spread for the Pilgrims first Thanksgiving. As for myself, I was content with one plate loaded with smothered steak, fried chicken and vegetables.

By the time I'd polished off one drumstick and a glass of ice tea, Joe Don was already back at the hot food counter loading up on more meat. Of course, he had to smoke a cigarette while he was getting another plate full of food. I had encouraged him to quit smoking, but worried that if he did and his appetite increased, he might jeopardize the city's food supply.

"I haven't been eating well lately," he told me moments later while wolfing down some brisket. "You know how it is when you get a divorce."

I reminded him that he'd been divorced for three years, that in that period of time he'd eaten a herd of cattle.

He grunted. "I don't care what you say, Mark, I've been off my feed lately."

Why Joe Don doesn't gain more weight, I just don't know. I'd sponsor him as a contestant in any eating contest, no matter what the menu.

After eating a couple of pieces of chocolate cake and a slab of pecan pie for dessert, Joe Don mellowed out and seemed anxious enough to discuss the man who called himself Jesus. He agreed that the man was probably the hairbrained idea of one of our mutual comedian friends. However, he didn't have a clue as to who it might be. I had dismissed Joe Don as a suspect, because he spent all his extra money on food and cigarettes. And by the time he paid child support, he didn't have any to squander on a joke.

By the time we got back to the police station, some of Joe Don's underlings had some reports on his inquiries about the man who called himself Jesus. The FBI had more than a dozen persons on file who claimed to be Jesus Christ, all politicians. The man who called himself Jesus was not on the list, nor were his fingerprints on file, anywhere.

"Sorry, pal," Joe Don said, "but nobody has anything on your man. Of course, that doesn't mean anything. There's still a few folks out there who aren't in a computer file."

"That's comforting," I said, sarcastically.

Joe Don grunted. "That's just like you. You're ready to start complaining about *Big Brother,* but you sure weren't hesitant to use *Big Brother* to find out the identity of the guy."

His statement pissed me off. I don't like being trapped by my own verbage any more than the next person. I asked Joe Don if he'd like to come over to the house on Sunday, play a little touch football, have lunch and watch the Dallas Cowboys on the tube.

"Who all's going to be there?" he asked.

I told him it would be the normal crew, the guys and gals who usually came over for one of these occasions.

"I'll come if you don't invite Sue Beth," he said.

The reference was to Sue Beth Larsen, a realtor by profession who at one time had the hots for Joe Don. He thought she was still after him, but Sue

Beth had assured me she had met her true love and no longer had any interest in Joe Don.

"Sue Beth doesn't give a damn about you," I said. "She's interested in a jockey she met a few months ago at Louisiana Downs." Louisiana Downs is a racetrack near Shreveport.

"Sue Beth and a jockey? You've got to be shitin' me."

"No, I'm serious."

"Mark, the woman weighs in at more than two hundred pounds. How much does this jockey weigh?"

I argued that Sue Beth did not weigh much more than two hundred pounds, and that she was tall.

"Hell, I know she's tall," Joe Don said, "which makes it even funnier. How tall is the jockey?"

"I think he's a little over five feet, and he weighs a little over a hundred pounds."

Joe Don guffawed. "Damn, she's almost a foot taller than him. I hope she doesn't roll over on him in bed. She'll flat-assed suffocate the little rascal."

While agreeing that Sue Beth and the jockey looked a bit comical together, I reminded Joe Don that she had been very nice to him. She had provided him a place to stay for a couple of months after his wife had booted him out of the house.

"Granted, she's a good-hearted woman," he said, still chuckling, "but I don't want her smothering me with affection."

"She's not going to bother you," I assured. "She's

crazy about the jockey. They plan to go in business together, build a race track here in the Dallas area."

Joe Don turned somber. "Oh, yeah, a lot of our legislators want parimutuel betting in Texas. They think that a lottery will fill up the state's coffers with money. Horse racing certainly has helped Louisiana and Arkansas. Now there's a couple of profitable states for you."

I didn't want to get into an argument with Joe Don on all the ill effects horse racing and other forms of gambling will allegedly bring to the state of Texas. That's one area where he's pure Baptist, though he hasn't darkened the door of a church in more than twenty years.

"Yeah," he ranted on, "Look how profitable gambling is for Atlantic City and New Mexico. There's a couple of real winners, too."

Joe Don's contention is that no matter how well-regulated gambling is in the state, it will still be run by organized crime. When I feel like arguing about it, I contend that organized crime is better equipped to run the state than the state legislature. Organized crime will at least show a profit. The crime is that the legislature never does, just squanders tax money without showing any return.

Of course, I could care less about horse racing. And I really agree with Joe Don that it ends up costing a state more than any benefits it provides. Joe Don is vehement in saying that where you have parimutuel betting, the crime rate increases dramatically. It's hard to argue with his statistics.

"I'm not going to argue parimutuel betting with you," I said. "I just want to know if you're coming over to the house Sunday?"

"What are you fixing?" he asked.

"I was thinking about barbecued spareribs."

"If you'll do more than think about it, you can count me in. Is the guy who calls himself Jesus going to be there?"

"That's one of the reasons I'm having this get-together," I answered. "I'm inviting all my alleged friends. That way, maybe I can find out which of them put the guy up to what he's doing."

VI

Ribs Davis is a man with a message, almost always emblazoned on the front of a T-shirt. Even on the coldest of days, Ribs exposes the front of his T-shirt, which normally carries a sterling message like GROCERY SACKERS DO IT BETTER or WHEN WATERMELONS ARE OUTLAWED, ONLY OUT-LAWS WILL HAVE WATERMELONS.

Ribs must have more than a hundred T-shirts, all with poignant messages like the aforementioned. He even has a KVIL SUCKS T-shirt.

For those who don't know, KVIL is the most pop-ular radio station in Dallas, which upsets Ribs to no end. He didn't always dislike the station, used to listen to it regularly. But now he thinks KVIL, and especially morning host Ron Chapman, has a ven-detta against him. His reasoning is based on the fact that he has never won any money from any of the station's contests.

Much of the time Rib's reasoning is like barbe-cue sauce gone bad.

I've never won any money from KVIL, either, but it's my favorite station and my car and home radios are tuned to it. That's something else Ribs doesn't like. On many occasions when he has been riding in my car, Ribs has threatened to get out and walk if I don't turn to another station. I generally stop the car and give him the opportunity to walk, but thus far he has never taken it.

Ribs, of course, tries to play on my sympathy, making the accusation that the reason he never wins anything from KVIL is because Ron Chapman doesn't like black people. I always reiterate that I haven't won anything either, and that I'm white. But reason and common sense aren't long suits with Ribs.

There are a number of reasons why Ribs' complaint about Ron Chapman doesn't hold water with me. For one thing, I've never heard Ron verbally attack persons from New York, Detroit or even California, so he must be a saintly man, therefore not a racist.

Besides, everyone pales in comparison to Ribs when it comes to being a racist. Collectively, Ribs doesn't like any race, religion, creed or color. He doesn't like black people, white people, yellow people, brown people, or any combination of colors. What's more, he doesn't even like barbecued spareribs, watermelon or soul food, all of which I crave. I often think the good Lord should have painted Ribs' face white, mine black.

When we're watching a football game on television, it's always Ribs who hollers out, "Look at that nigger carrying the ball like a watermelon." And it's always Ribs who is saying that the reason there are so few black quarterbacks in the NFL is because no black man wants to pass something shaped like a watermelon to someone else.

Ribs never pays any attention to my complaints about his racism. Instead, he flaunts it. He even tried to join the Klu Klux Klan because he thought the uniforms were neat. This is the same guy who complains about department stores having WHITE SALES.

I've already said that some of Ribs' more intelligent communication is on his T-shirts. He also has a collection of *gimme* caps that must run into the thousands. These caps advertise everything from cow manure to artificial insemination.

I'm eternally grateful that Ribs always wears such caps like a baseball catcher, with the bill at the back of his head. About the only way to see the cap's advertisement, if someone wanted to, is to stand behind him.

One of these caps is always perched on his head, as important a part of his wardrobe as a T-shirt.

You'd think with the T-shirts and *gimme* caps that Ribs would wear jeans and running shoes. But no, he usually wears expensive slacks, wingtip lace shoes, and ultrasuede sports jackets. Like Billy Bob Raintree, Ribs thinks he's making a fashion statement.

Before you get the wrong idea, I'm not one of those persons who goes around saying, "Some of my best friends are black." Ribs is about the only black person with whom I associate, and I think our rather loose-knit friendship is based more on his athletic ability than anything else.

I met Ribs a few years ago when at a park playing touch football with some of the guys. My team was short a man and I noticed Ribs standing on the sideline looking baleful, something he does as well as anyone I've ever met. Anyway, I invited him to play with us and he reluctantly agreed.

I recall saying to him, "You look like a split end to me."

The statement drew a suspicious look and the questioning response, "What you mean?"

"Split end is a position in football," I explained.

"Oh."

"Anyway, you're tall and lanky," I continued. "A lot of split ends are tall and lanky."

"I kind of want to play center," he said.

Bobo Harrison grunted out, "I'm the center." Bobo likes to play center because it requires little, if any, running. At least, that's the way Bobo plays the position. Because he always has a can of beer in one hand, Bobo is a one-handed snapper, even though we always operate from a punt formation. Bobo's center snaps are a little erratic, but that helps keep everyone alert.

Ribs took one look at Bobo and decided he wanted to be a split end. It was a wise decision, primarily because we were using Bobo's ball. If he hadn't been allowed to play center, he would have taken his ball and gone home. As soon as all the beer was gone, of course. Bobo can be pretty immature at times.

Anyway, when in the huddle I told Ribs to run a fly pattern. He glanced down at his crotch and again suspiciously asked, "Say what?"

"No, no," I said, then patiently with an index finger drew the play on the ground. Ribs nodded as though he understood, but when looking in his eyes I saw that no one was home.

When Bobo snapped the ball to me, Ribs sprinted downfield and I lofted a pass in his direction. He caught the ball when in full stride, but instead of tucking it away and running, he suddenly started trying to dribble it toward the goal line.

"No, no," I screamed, running down the field in his direction.

Ribs obviously realized his mistake, because he looked at me sheepishly and said, "Sorry man, but when a black man gets a ball in his hands, his instincts make him want to dribble it."

At the time, I thought ol' Ribs might just be putting me on. But as I came to know him better, I discovered that Ribs danced to the beat of a different drummer. Nothing brought that home better than learning he was taking accordion and polka lessons, and that his dream is to become another Lawrence Welk.

I told him I thought it a little strange that a black man would want to play the accordion and dance the polka, but his reasoning is that if Charley Pride can be a country-western singer, anything is possible. I don't understand the connection, but there's a lot about Ribs that I don't understand.

Once trained not to dribble the football after catching it, Ribs has become one of my team's best pass receivers. And for a man who wears wingtip lace-up shoes on the football field, he is amazingly fast and agile, makes cuts that would be the envy of an NFL receiver.

Ribs lives in an apartment on the north side of town, close to my house. He has lived there ever since I've known him, but is always threatening to move because of what he terms *gross discrimination.* He contends the management is racist because no other black people live in the complex.

The apartment complex's management has assured him to the contrary, even offered to give him a deduction in rent if he can get other blacks to move into their apartments. But with one breath he claims management is patronizing him, and with another he's telling me that he doesn't want to live in a place where there are a bunch of niggers.

"If there were a bunch of niggers living over there, nothing I have would be safe," he said. "Niggers will lie and steal."

I've often told Ribs that a person doesn't have to be black to be a nigger.

For a while, Ribs got on a kick where he wanted to date a white girl. He kept asking white girls out and got turned down so much he began to think he was like covers on a bed. Finally, a white girl did agree to go out with him, but Ribs broke the date.

"I can't have any respect for a white woman who would go out with a black man," he told me.

Ribs is, indeed, hard to figure.

When I first met Ribs, he was trying to make it as a stock broker. His success in the field was mediocre at best, something he attributed to the fact that no white man was going to trust a black man to invest his money. As for handling stock transactions for blacks, he said he couldn't even get blacks to invest in watermelon futures.

"If a black man doesn't have the money in his pocket," Ribs said, "he doesn't believe he has the money."

If a college diploma means anything, Ribs is an educated man. He graduated from an all-black college, but now thinks all such schools should be closed. He laughs at television commercials promoting all-black colleges, especially the ones with the theme *A Mind is a Terrible Thing to Waste.* Ribs says the best place to waste a mind is in an all-black school.

More than once he has said to me, "It must be tough for you to understand, how it's okay for us to have all-black schools but it's not okay for you people to have all-white schools."

He contends that all-black schools promote racism, and that anyone with severe learning disabilities attending an all-black school has a good chance to graduate with honors.

"My degree is from Farce University," he often says.

When I tried to tell Ribs he has a lot of native intelligence, his response was, "Like in African."

Ribs tried his hand at driving a DART bus, but that didn't last too long. He said it was just too lonely driving an empty vehicle, never having any passengers. He contends the only reason for DART buses is to haul domestic help from south to north Dallas.

So, while he's waiting for his shot at becoming the new polka king, Ribs is selling used cars. He says it's pretty easy to unload old Cadillacs, Buicks and Pontiacs on *the brothers*. And he sells quite a few Chevrolets to illegal aliens.

As for Ribs' wheels, he drives a Volkswagen convertible.

It was late Wednesday afternoon when I encountered Ribs in front of my house. I had gone out to retrieve the mail from my box and, as is always the case, discovered Ribs out walking his dog Blackie. It should be mentioned here that Blackie is a redbone hound, about as red in color as a dog can be. Ribs once told me the reason he named the dog Blackie was because he didn't want to name him Indian.

"But he's as black-hearted as the meanest Indian on earth," Ribs said.

Blackie is your typical hound, fairly unconcerned about the world around him. When Ribs is talking about him, the dog always looks bemused.

Anyway, I think Ribs plans his Wednesday evening walk with Blackie for about the time he knows I'll be retrieving the mail. Both of us take off a little early from work on Wednesdays. I've often thought Ribs and Blackie hide in the bushes until I come out of the house, because they're as regular on Wednesday evenings as a morning constitutional.

As to why, it's because I always invite Ribs to have dinner with me. He has had dinner with me every Wednesday evening from the first week I met him, except for when I've been on vacation. And always, he just happen by. I've tried to make it just a standing invitation, but he doesn't want to tie himself down.

"Do you and Blackie want to have dinner with me?" I asked.

Ribs looked at Blackie and asked, "You want to have dinner with ol' Mark, Blackie?"

The dog gave Ribs that bemused look, which he interpreted to be a yes. Then Ribs asked, "What are we having, Mark?"

"Fried chicken, jalapeno blackeyed peas and cornbread." It is the same thing we have every Wednesday. Blackie always has a large can of Alpo Beef Dinner, which I stock for these Wednesday rituals.

"Sounds good to me," Ribs said, as though the menu was something exciting and new.

While we were gorging ourselves with fried chicken and peas, and Blackie was wolfing down his Alpo, I told Ribs about the man who called himself Jesus.

"Where is he now?" Ribs asked.

"It being Wednesday evening, I guess he went to church," I replied.

"That's a good sign."

"Anyway, I want to have a get-together here on Sunday and you can meet him," I continued.

"Blackie and I are planning on going coon hunting Saturday night, so I might be a little tired on Sunday," Ribs said.

Ribs' affinity for hunting raccoons all night is something I've never understood, but it's serious sport for him. Blackie is a registered coon dog and Ribs is a member of the American Coon Hunters Association. He has an American Coon Hunters belt buckle, jacket patch and membership card. And he sports an American Coon Hunters decal and bumper sticker on his car.

"We're going to eat, watch the game and then play a little touch," I said, "so I hope you can come."

"I just said I might be tired, but I'll be here," Ribs assured. "Tell me, is this guy who calls himself Jesus black."

"No."

"Then I doubt if he's the real thing."

VII

Mary Lou Magruder and Sue Beth Larsen are close friends, which has always seemed a bit strange to me since Mary Lou basically detests women who work in real estate. Of course, Mary Lou still pictures women realtors as wearing white mid-calf boots, low-cut sweaters and flashy jewelry, which was common in Dallas several years ago.

It's still, I suppose, easy enough to spot women realtors in a bar. They usually run in herds, hold their cigarettes a certain way, drink too much and talk too loud. And they do dress a certain way, look a certain way, talk a certain way.

Anyway, Mary Lou isn't fond of women realtors, except for Sue Beth, who doesn't look like a realtor. If anything, Sue Beth looks like a mud wrestler.

Sue Beth has been very successful in real estate. She has a Mercedes and a Cadillac, alternates days in driving the two vehicles. She also has a monster house out near the Willow Bend Polo Club, a house that's valued at either seven figures or close to it.

But Sue Beth doesn't take great pains with her appearance. She thinks diet is simply a four-letter word for whatever she wants to eat, and she wants to eat plenty. She can down a two-pound porterhouse steak with all the trimmings before a race horse can run a quarter mile. And if she gets her hands on a carton of ice cream, whether pint, quart or gallon, she'll eat it all.

Of course, I can't fault her for the ice cream. It affects me the same way.

Sue Beth never admits to being fat. She claims that she is just big boned, which is like saying an elephant isn't heavy. Make no mistake about it, Sue Beth is big. And fat.

Someone once told me that most fat people are jovial, and Sue Beth certainly fits the bill on that score. She seems to find the whole world amusing. All her skinnier peers have those phony laughs, but Sue Beth's laughter is genuine, robust and infectious. Maybe it's just harder to be happy when you're dieting to be skinny, when you're doing all that exercise. Sue Beth's idea of exercise is getting out of her car to buy a family-size bucket of Kentucky Fried Chicken, which for her is a bedtime snack.

Someone also told me that rich people aren't really happy. I'd like to give it a shot, because I don't know any poor people who are happy, either. And Sue Beth certainly doesn't seem to have any problem enjoying her wealth.

Maybe Sue Beth's secret to happiness is that she's a half-assed psychic, or at least claims to be. She makes about as much cash reading tea leaves as she does selling property. Hundreds of divorced female realtors in Dallas worship at her feet, trying to get her to tell them that *Mr. Right* is about to enter their life.

I figure if Sue Beth wants to play psychic, it's okay with me. As far as I'm concerned, she can practice voodoo. I like the woman because she's a genuinely caring person, but one who likes a practical joke. And I figured she might just be the one who initiated the Jesus joke, probably with devious Mary Lou's help. For that reason, I asked Sue Beth and Mary Lou to meet me for drinks Thursday evening.

We met at Andrew's, a nice little spot on McKinney. It offers a kind of cozy atmosphere, a particularly unique ambiance.

Mary Lou was her usual charming sarcastic self, making reference to the fact that she felt extremely privileged to be in my company twice in a one-week period.

"If you want to come over Sunday, you can make it three times," I said. "I'm having everyone over to eat, watch the game and play a little touch football. Both of you are invited."

"Sunday is the beginning of a new week," Mary Lou informed.

I gave her my best sneer, which prompted Sue Beth to say, "You two really ought to get back together. You argue and fuss beautifully."

I grunted. "If I wanted to go through Marine boot camp, I could get paid for it."

We were all enjoying our favorite libations. I was having my usual frozen margarita, Mary Lou was having a wine spritzer and Sue Beth was sucking on a longneck bottle of beer. Sue Beth is not pretentious.

"Has Mark told you about his house guest?" Mary Lou asked Sue Beth.

Sue Beth finished chewing a bite of hamburger, swallowed and replied, "No, he hasn't. Who is this house guest of yours, Mark?"

"The guy claims to be Jesus Christ," I said.

She laughed. "Jesus Christ in your house? Jesus Christ as your running buddy? I don't think so."

Irritated, I said, "You act as though if he was Jesus Christ, he wouldn't have anything to do with me."

"Right," Mary Lou agreed. "I can't understand why anyone who even poses as Jesus Christ would have anything to do with you."

"You weren't quite so sarcastic when we were having breakfast the other morning."

"That's because you caught me on a bad day," she said. "I was feeling all melancholy."

"You should try melancholy more often," I suggested. "It's more becoming."

"About this guy who calls himself Jesus," Sue Beth said, "fill me in on what's going on."

"I figured *The Mouth* here had already told you," I replied. "Or I figured you might have sent him my way."

"Why would I do that?"

"It beats the hell out of me," I answered. "But you have been known to play a practical joke or two, Sue Beth. And it sounds like some hairbrained idea that you and Mary Lou would cook up."

"I swear," she said, "that I know nothing about it. And Mary Lou hasn't told me about it, because we haven't talked this week. I just got back from Louisiana."

"Over to see your jockey friend?" I asked.

"Yes."

"How is he?"

She beamed. "He's wonderful."

Now I have to say that Sue Beth's as hard to read as Billy Bob Raintree, but for a different reason. Billy Bob is just flat cunning, but Sue Beth's eyes are always laughing. They're laughing when she's playing a joke and when she isn't.

"How's ol' Chigger doing?" I asked. Sue Beth's jockey friend is Chigger Dodgen, who isn't a household word among racing fans. "You can bring him over to the house on Sunday if you like."

"He can't," she replied, sorrowfully. "He has his children for the weekend and has to stay in Louisiana. They're going to pick up aluminum cans to earn some Christmas money."

From what I'd been able to learn, the little guy had conned Sue Beth out of several hundred thousand in just a few months. But I couldn't help but admire his approach.

"He sounds like a wonderful man, a real Fred Crachet," I said. Out of the corner of one of my eyes, I saw Mary Lou roll hers.

"He is," Sue Beth affirmed.

"How many children does he have?" I asked.

"Twelve."

"The little rascal's been busy. He must have worn his wife out."

"Not really," she said. "He's been married twelve times, and he has a child from each of his marriages."

I couldn't help but chuckle. "So you're going to be number thirteen?"

"I hope so."

"I don't think there's any doubt about it," I assured. "And I hope you have a long and happy marriage."

Sue Beth laughed. "I know you find it amusing, Chigger having had twelve wives."

"Now what makes you think that, Sue Beth?"

"You forget, Mark, I know you. You can laugh if you want, but I think Chigger's really ready to settle down."

"Hey, I'm envious of ol' Chigger's record," I said. "What's the longest he's been married to any of these women?"

"He was married fourteen months to his last wife."

"And that's the longest he was married to any of them?"

"Chigger's been on the road a lot," she explained.

I figured Chigger was the only guy I knew about who needed a computer to keep track of his children. And he needed a purse, not a wallet, in which to carry pictures of them.

"I kind of hate to ask this, Sue Beth, but are you and Chigger planning to have any children?"

"We've talked about it," she said.

I checked Mary Lou out and said, "You've been awfully quiet."

"Is there anything in particular you want me to say?" she asked.

"No, I just thought you might be interested in Sue Beth and Chigger."

"I am interested in Sue Beth and Chigger," she said. "It's just that I know everything she's told you."

Sue Beth went back to eating her hamburger. Actually, it was her third hamburger.

"And what do you think of this union?" I asked Mary Lou.

"If it makes Sue Beth happy, I think it's wonderful."

"Well, I guess we can both agree on that."

Sue Beth reprimanded us with, "You two hush. I've never seen two people who cared as much about each other fight so much."

Mary Lou glanced back across her shoulder, like she thought Sue Beth was talking to someone behind her, then asked, "Are you talking to me?"

Sue Beth laughed, continued working on her hamburger and longneck.

"Mark, go ahead and tell Sue Beth about meeting the man who calls himself Jesus," Mary Lou said.

"I think she probably already knows."

"No, I really don't," Sue Beth said.

What the hell, it didn't matter. I started telling Sue Beth about the man who called himself Jesus, every single detail from the time I first met him on Sunday night. She seemed genuinely fascinated with the story, interrupted only long enough to order two more hamburgers and a couple of longneck bottles of beer.

I finished with, "You being psychic and all, Sue Beth, you ought to be able to tell me who the man really is."

She shook her head in resignation, reached in her purse and took out a pair of dark glasses. She put them on and said, "If I had something that belonged to the man, I might be able to help you. The only problem is, Mark, that I know you don't believe in psychic phenomena."

Sue Beth always puts on the dark glasses when she goes into her psychic routine. It's hard to be accepted as a serious psychic when you have laughing eyes. Most of Sue Beth's believers have never seen her when she didn't have the glasses on.

"I believe in bullshit, Sue Beth, so why do you

say I don't believe in psychic phenomena?"

Mary Lou came on with, "That's the trouble with you, Mark, you think you're so damn smart."

"Hey, cut me some slack, Sugar, I'm just kidding." Mary Lou doesn't like to be called Sugar, which is why I call her Sugar.

While Mary Lou seethed, Sue Beth pondered and then acted as though she was in a trance. It might have worked if the waiter hadn't arrived with the hamburgers. The smell of the burgers obviously broke the spell, because she was soon chomping down on one and taking periodic swigs from a longneck bottle of beer.

"The setting is wrong here," she said. "When I come over to your house on Sunday, then I can tell more about the man from his aura. He will be there, won't he?"

"As far as I know."

"Who else is going to be there?"

"The usual bunch."

"Including Joe Don?"

"Yeah, he's planning on being there."

"That does present a problem," she said.

"Why's that?"

"Well, you know that Joe Don is crazy about me."

I knew that Joe Don thought Sue Beth was crazy about him, but her revelation regarding his feelings for her was new to me. I shrugged my shoulders and said, "I think you can handle it."

"Oh, I know I can handle it," she said, "but I really don't want to hurt him."

"Hey," I said, suddenly enjoying the dialogue even more, "he's a big boy. He's going to have to learn to deal with heartache and rejection. You owe it to him to explain your feelings for Chigger."

Mary Lou, I knew, was angry at me for teasing Sue Beth. But Sue Beth was as serious as a DART bus driver is about his afternoon nap.

"Do you think I should talk to him?"

"I think you should," I replied. "Maybe you can get the guy who calls himself Jesus to help you."

VIII

Chico Neiman Marcus is another guy who just sort of showed up one day and started playing touch football with us. He lives in the same apartment complex where Ribs lives.

Chico is Mexican, of course, but decided to change his name when he went into the retail business. His real name is Sergio Vicente Martinez Dominquez, thus the name Chico.

As to why Chico decided to use the name Neiman Marcus, he reasons that it is a way to establish some identity with the famous Neiman-Marcus stores. I've never thought Chico's clients were that concerned with image. He's in the used hubcap business.

I've asked Chico many times where he gets the *new* used hubcaps that he sells. And he always tells me that people just bring them in.

"A hubcap shop is kind of like a pawn shop," Chico told me.

"How's that?" I asked. "Do you make loans on hubcaps?"

"No, no loans."

"Then how is it like a pawn shop?"

"Just trust me," he said.

I will say this for Chico. When the hubcaps on my new BMW came up missing, he was *Johnny-on-the-spot* with a new set, and at half the price charged by a dealer. It was a convenient purchase, too, since Chico had a set in the trunk of his car.

Chico's business is operated out of an old building on Harry Hines, a section of Dallas where there are a lot of porno shops and photography studios where you can rent a camera and a model for thirty minutes to an hour. The area attracts a lot of artists and ladies in tight, short skirts who do a lot of walking up and down the street in spike heel shoes.

The building where Chico displays his hubcaps was a Texaco service station many years ago, but the only evidence of its past glory is a faded Fram oil filter sign. The frame building was white, but the paint is yellowing, weathered and peeling. The whole place would be a real challenge for Sears Weatherbeater paint.

Chico has started painting the building, has about a fourth of it done. I can't say much for his choice of colors, which are pink and blue-green. Chico has also expanded his product line to include velvet paintings, pottery and blankets, and Mexican dresses, which he buys in Mexico for twelve dollars each and sells for forty.

The man is no dummy when it comes to merchandising. He buys cheap, sells high.

The guy Chico hired to paint the sign for his store misspelled a couple of words: The sign reads:

KNEEMAN-MARCOS HUBCAP & DISCOUNT CENTER. I told Chico he ought to make the guy redo the sign, but he uttered what he considered to be a profound statement. "What is written is written."

As for Chico, he is a short, wiry man who has no Mexican accent, except when it's beneficial to him. He was, of course, born in Dallas, attended public schools here and even got an associates degree from El Centro College, which is part of the Dallas County Community College District.

Philosophically, he is totally opposed to illegal aliens, thinks they represent a real threat to the Texas economy. He's always saying that if he had lived during the Texas Revolution, he would have been fighting alongside Travis at the Alamo. For people from New York and Detroit who don't know, Travis commanded the troops at the Alamo. Those who don't know about the Alamo need to get a book and read up on it.

Chico gets fighting mad when Bobo says, "Travis wouldn't have had you, you little shit." If Chico's face wasn't so brown, I'm sure it would turn red. Maybe it does, but the brown hides it.

Anyway, after the man who called himself Jesus came home on Wednesday night from what I ascertained was another disappointing visit to a local church, we started talking about his job prospects. He was doing a heckuva job cleaning up the house, but I didn't think the work was too fulfilling.

task and simply set up a time for Chico to meet the man who called himself Jesus. We decided to meet at eight o'clock Friday morning at the Mecca Cafe, one of the more famous eating establishments on Harry Hines.

The Mecca Cafe is decorated in University of Texas and University of Oklahoma memorabilia, though some misguided individual inadvertently stuck a Texas A&M University decal on one of the restaurant's walls. The waitresses are forever having to apologize for it, but no one has taken it on themselves to remove it.

What the Mecca Cafe specializes in is down home cooking, some of the best food in Dallas. It's not fancy dining, but it puts a lot of the city's more pretentious restaurants to shame in terms of good taste. Good taste to me is what goes in my mouth, not how things are decorated or where they are located.

The man who called himself Jesus and I arrived at the Mecca a few minutes after Chico, who had already entrenched himself in a booth. I introduced employer and potential employee to each other, and then we ordered breakfast.

The man who called himself Jesus ordered grits with his eggs and biscuits, which made me feel a little better about him. He also asked for a side order of cream gravy.

While we were all sipping our coffee, Chico said, "Mark tells me you call yourself Jesus."

Ribs had already left the house, but during the course of dinner, while he was finishing off the last of the jalapeno blackeyed peas and cornbread, he mentioned that Chico was looking for some help.

"Of course, you never can tell about the little spic, whether he's lying or not," Ribs said. "He likes to act like he's running some kind of big conglomerate instead of something several notches below a Goodwill store."

Ribs and Blackie weren't there when the man who called himself Jesus got in from church, so what I told him about Chico's need for help was even more secondhand than what Ribs had told me. The man seemed pretty excited about the job prospect, though, even when I told him it wasn't in one of the better sections of town.

So it was on Thursday, before I met Sue Beth and Mary Lou for drinks, that I had called Chico and asked him to interview the man. When I told Chico the man called himself Jesus, his response was, "He's not some illegal alien from Mexico or Puerto Rico, is he?"

I assured him that the man was not an illegal alien, though I wasn't entirely sure of my facts, and then tried to explain the difference in the U.S. relationship to Mexico and Puerto Rico.

"Yeah, yeah," Chico said. "I don't care what you say, all these greasers are the same."

Though I continued trying to explain, I soon grew tired with the futility of my self-appointed

"That's right," the man replied.

"There are lots of people named Jesus in Mexico," Chico continued. "Of course, they pronounce it Hay-Suice there. You're not from Mexico, are you?"

The man smiled. "In a sense you could say I'm from everywhere."

"Do you speak Mexican?" Chico asked.

"I speak all languages," was the soft response.

Chico looked at me, and I could see the suspicion in his eyes. "All languages, huh?"

"That's correct."

"Well, that's a definite plus," Chico said. "Mostly we get Mexicans who can't speak American, but we also get some people from New York, Chicago and Detroit. Can you speak their language, too?"

The man who called himself Jesus chuckled. "Like I said, I speak all languages."

"Mark also told me you claim to be the Jesus of the New Testament."

"That's also correct."

Chico looked at the man closely, then gave a negative shake of the head. "Well, you sure don't look like any pictures of Jesus that I've ever seen."

The man chuckled again. "It's a shame the writers of the New Testament didn't have photographs to illustrate their work, but cameras weren't available at the time."

"I don't know about that," Chico said, "but my mother has a Bible that's full of pictures. And down at the store I've got a picture of Jesus on black velvet that doesn't look anything like you."

The man who called himself Jesus shook his head in resignation. "Artists have always been strange."

Fortunately, breakfast arrived and I had the opportunity to work on some biscuits, ham, gravy and grits. And even with his mouth full, Chico continued questioning the man who called himself Jesus. "Do you have any experience in hubcap sales?" he wanted to know.

"Experience?" I questioned. "Just how many people in the world do you think have experience in hubcap sales?"

Chico shrugged his shoulders. "How should I know? And if you're so damn smart, Mark, what kind of questions would you ask somebody you might hire to sell hubcaps?"

"I can't answer that because you're the only hubcap salesman I know."

"Well, until you can come up with some better questions," he said, "don't criticize me for the ones I ask." Then, directing his words to the man who called himself Jesus, Chico asked, "What do you think your strong suits are?"

"First and foremost, I'm honest," the man said.

Chico gave that negative shake of the head again. "I'm not sure that's a strong suit."

"You don't want someone who would steal from you, do you?" I asked.

Chico again gave his classic shrug of the shoulders. "It doesn't matter, I've got that built into my price structure."

"Even if you do," I argued, "I wouldn't think you'd want someone stealing from you."

"Maybe you're right," he said, "but up until now I've been my only employee. It doesn't matter if I steal from me."

When Ribs and Chico get together, you can imagine the kind of logic that spews forth like a geyser. Both Plato and Aristotle would be overwhelmed.

For the next few minutes, the conversation was not that memorable. I did suggest that Chico join us on Sunday to eat, watch the ball game and play a little touch football. He thought it was a wonderful idea, as long as we weren't having Mexican food, which he claims to dislike. I asked the man who called himself Jesus if he was going to be there. He assured his attendance, but said it would have to be after church was over. I suggested he catch an early service to be sure he didn't miss any of the game.

The several cups of coffee I'd had were begging for release, so I excused myself and went to the john, leaving Chico with the man who called himself Jesus. When I came out of the john, I noted they were engaged in heavy conversation, which diminished as I approached the table.

"Well, did you decide to hire J.C. here?" I asked.

Chico looked at me with obvious distaste, then

said, "I don't think you need to be using initials for Jesus Christ. I'm not sure it's proper."

"What the . . ."

"It doesn't matter," the man who called himself Jesus said.

"It matters to me," Chico chimed. "And yes, Mark, I have hired Jesus here. I don't think he'll have any trouble catching on to hubcap sales. In fact, I don't think he'll have any trouble selling any of the quality merchandise I have in my store."

"Great," I grunted. "When does he start?"

"Right now," was the reply. "As soon as we have another cup of coffee or two and you pay the check."

"How are you going to get home this evening?" I asked the man who called himself Jesus. "Do you want me to pick you up?"

"I'll give him a ride home," Chico said. "Don't worry about it."

I wasn't planning to worry about it, but was glad that Chico had volunteered. I was hoping I might get lucky with a chick who had just started working at the paper, but more than that I was happy at not having to drive back to Harry Hines.

When we left the Mecca and walked to Chico's car, I closely observed the man who called himself Jesus. I expected some kind of reaction from him when he saw Chico's car, but he was as expression-less as a smooth rock.

Chico's anti-Mexican sentiment doesn't include cars. He has a Chevrolet with its rear end jacked up so high that it looks as though the front end is crashing into whatever surface is before it. The car is painted purple and yellow, and its interior is done in some sort of fuzzy red cloth, including the dashboard. There's a plastic Jesus on the dashboard, big cloth dice hanging from the rear view mirror, and a waggy-headed dog behind the back seat and looking out the rear window.

The car deserves a spot in the *Smithsonian,* perhaps a segment on the television version of *Ripley's Believe It Or Not.* Anyway, I watched it until it was out of sight, and wondered how the man who called himself Jesus would do in his first day as a hubcap salesman.

IX

It never occurred to me that Chico might be the brains behind the man who called himself Jesus. It's not that he isn't capable of a practical joke, it's just that the Jesus scenario is not his style. Besides, Chico is so wrapped up in thinking about hubcaps that I doubt he has time to think of anything else. With him, hubcaps are an obsession.

Needless to say, the new chick at the paper told me where I could stick my invitation for an after work drink, so I called Bobby Jack Lewis and asked him to join me. Bobby Jack owns the Apocalypse Now Dating Service, but never seems to be able to get a date. He lies well, though, always tells me he'll join me if he can break away from Sue, Jane, Polly, or Belinda. He uses a lot of other female names, too, all fictitious in terms of a relationship or date with him. I play the game because it doesn't hurt, allow him to think that I believe he is covered up with women.

But Bobby Jack is always able to break away from any fictional girlfriend with whom he allegedly has a date. Not once have I ever worried that he wouldn't meet me for a drink. Thus far, he has never failed to show up, always with a silly grin and a story about how he practically had to hire a winch truck to pull his date off him. Always, I tell him he should have brought her along. And always, he tells me he doesn't want a bimbo hanging on him while he's having a drink with a pal.

All Bobby Jack's fictional girlfriends are bimbos. In fact, to Bobby Jack's way of thinking, all women are bimbos. That's why he doesn't like to be around Mary Lou Magruder. Her IQ is a good fifty points higher than his, so she intimidates him.

From a strictly religious perspective, Bobby Jack had to rank as a prime suspect in terms of responsibility for the man who called himself Jesus. Bobby Jack had, after all, been born to religious parents, people of the cloth. Bobby Jack's father was a Jewish rabbi, who fell in love with and married a Catholic nun.

Both had to reject their callings for the love affair to continue, but there was really no choice. Bobby Jack was already on the way before the marriage could even be consummated.

With no place to turn, Bobby Jack's father accepted the Christian faith and became an immediate success as an evangelist. Protestants turned out in droves to see and hear a man who had seen the light, who had rejected the Jewish faith. He was almost as popular as an athlete who rejects sin and gives his Christian testimony, or a man saved from drugs or drunkedness.

Bobby Jack's mother experienced equal religious

success, being able to finally give her testimony on the evils of Rome.

With such a dynamic mother and father, both evangelical zealots, it seemed normal enough that Bobby Jack would follow in their footsteps. By the time he was three-years-old, Bobby Jack was standing on a stool behind a pulpit giving his Christian testimony. True, speech was somewhat difficult for him at such a young age, but many of his utterances were hailed as being the unknown tongue. Bobby Jack was a charismatic, something that deserted him when he entered the first grade.

With his father on the road winning souls, the burden of bringing Bobby Jack up in the way fell heavily upon his mother's shoulders. She was equal to the task, never allowing Bobby Jack to miss any church service, or Vacation Bible School, for eighteen years. Except for that period of time when he was in the closet.

Bobby Jack and his parents made their home in a small and forgettable Texas town, one whose name and location he can't even remember. Bobby Jack can't go home again because he doesn't know where it is, which is why he hasn't seen his parents on holidays for twenty-five years.

Anyway, Bobby Jack was somewhat of a celebrity in the town, him being a youthful charismatic and his father being an evangelist and all. His mother added to his celebrity status because she, being a very frugal woman, still wore her old habits to the grocery store and some church events.

Bobby Jack vaguely recalls a lawsuit against his mother, the plaintiff being the Pope and the entire Catholic Church. Her crime was that of posing as a nun in nuns clothing. She was supposedly vindicated and cleared of the charges, one of the first televised cases heard by Judge Wapner on People's Court.

Anyway, the sure sign of a kid's popularity at Bobby Jack's school was being beaten up, according to Bobby Jack. Since he was beat up almost daily, he was one of the most popular kids in school.

Bobby Jack was never into drugs as a youth, but he was often stoned with real rocks. At the time, he thought such atrocities were just another burden for a Christian to bear.

The town where Bobby Jack was raised was farming country, the primary crop being oil. In fact, there were oil wells pumping at the end of his school's football field. The very first time he saw the field, something clicked in his mind. You see, Bobby Jack is somewhat of a proportional genius, and the field looked wrong to him.

One moonlit night, he took his ruler out to the field and measured it, discovered that the playing surface was only ninety yards long. What's more, he found that the ten-yard markers on the field were only nine yards apart.

Armed with this information, he went to the school's coach in hopes of ingratiating himself and getting good grades in physical education. But the coach became angry, told Bobby Jack that his twelve-inch ruler was an inch short, that the field was the proper length.

Because of his proportional genius, Bobby Jack begged to disagree, told the coach he planned to preach about the short field the following Sunday. He had already preached on the evils of the PTA-sponsored school carnival, and on a baseball catcher wearing a plastic cup inside his jockey strap.

Bobby Jack has always been one to speak out on the more pressing issues.

Anyway, the coach became irate and locked Bobby Jack inside one of the gym closets, told him he would have to stay there until the season was over. It wasn't something Bobby Jack wanted to hear, because this all happened prior to the first game of a ten-game schedule.

Timing has always been one of Bobby Jack's problems.

As for his folks worrying about him, the coach simply telephoned Bobby Jack's mother and told her that her son was going on an eleven-week physical education field trip. And because folks in a small Texas town never question a high school football coach's authority, Bobby Jack's mother just said "Fine" and continued counting her beads.

For Bobby Jack, life inside the gym closet was not that bad. Initially, he did complain about the bowl of gruel the coach brought him every day, so the coach started bringing him a tray of food from the school cafeteria. After two days of school cafeteria food, Bobby Jack asked the coach to start bringing the gruel again.

Bobby Jack was not alone inside the closet. He made friends with an old football, an old basketball, two roaches and a spider. For several years after leaving his hometown, before he forgot its name and location, Bobby Jack corresponded with the old football.

Timing is everything and Bobby Jack never had any. The year the coach locked him in the gym closet was the year the football team went to state, meaning they had to play five additional games. This meant a few more weeks in the closet for Bobby Jack. The coach forgot to call his mother to tell her the physical education field trip had been extended, but it didn't matter because she had forgotten he had called in the first place.

Bobby Jack's mother and father never worried when they didn't see their boy. They just figured it was an answer to prayer.

Nor did his teachers ever count him absent or give him anything other than good grades. They weren't about to put themselves in the position of having Bobby Jack in their class for another year.

The time Bobby Jack spent in the closet was a time of reflection and deep meditation. It was while he was in the closet that he began to ponder the real mysteries of life, why a man could purse his lips and tongue a certain way and emit a whistle. He was pretty sure no one else had given the subject much thought, which was why he prepared a series of sermons on his discovery. He titled the sermons, *Will There Be A Whistle Before The Second Coming?*

Bobby Jack thought about going to Baylor University to study for the ministry, but decided the ministry didn't require any study. Besides, he was already a full-fledged preacher, had even been a charismatic at one time. About the only challenge left was to find the right formula for a television ministry, and he thought he could better do that with a degree from Texas A&M. He also figured he could be more a missionary at A&M than at Baylor. He would attempt to get the Aggies to lay down their tall boots with spurs, their whips and swords, to perhaps beat them into plowshares. And he had heard so many stories of Aggies and animals. At the time, females were taboo at the school.

Another factor was that A&M offered a degree in proportions, which I've already established is one of Bobby Jack's strong suits. Anyway, he fit right in at A&M, was an honor graduate.

Deep down, though, I think he has always regretted not going to Baylor. I know he likes Waco, especially the one tall building in the city. It reminds him of a giant middle finger pointing skyward.

After graduation from A&M, Bobby Jack kind of lost his way. He couldn't get a job in proportions, which he blames on the state's disproportionate concern with numbers. He thinks too many people, namely Yankees, were allowed to cross the Red River and settle in Texas. Of course, he prefers Yankees to Iranians, but who doesn't?

Bobby Jack is always asking the question, "Why can't drivers education and sex education be taught on the same day in Iran?" The answer is that it's too hard on the camel.

The real tragedy of Bobby Jack not being able to get a job in proportions lies in the fact that he lost his confidence in God. He didn't get mad at God or anything like that, just reasoned that asking God to like an Aggie was too much to ask. And he also couldn't find a vacant time slot for another television evangelist.

So somewhere along the line, he just gave up preaching, primarily because no one would listen to him. I've encouraged him, told him that hasn't stopped anyone else. But he won't listen to me. I still think he is a closet preacher. But I can't think of a soul, including me, who wants him to come out of the closet.

As for the dating service, I suppose it's a living. I'm not sure how much Bobby Jack likes it, but he puts up a good front. He claims it's the best thing that ever happened to him, mainly because of all the broads who are hot and heavy after him, which is sheer fantasy on his part.

If Bobby Jack was a foot taller and handsome, he

would look like Robert Redford. The problem is that he's short and ugly, which is something I can't hold against him. I'm just taller.

Anyway, I said he had the background to pull the Jesus joke on me, but I really didn't consider him a suspect. He's a guy who, when he says darn, looks up expecting lightning to hit him. And though he meets me for a drink, he doesn't partake of spirits. He won't even buy a soft drink from the bar. He carries an Igloo cooler with him at all times, and it usually contains anywhere from three to six iced down strawberry soda pops. He says he can't get strawberry soda pop at a bar, which is probably true.

Bobby Jack met me at the Harvey House on Midway Road. He entered the place carrying his little cooler and plopped down on the chair across from me.

"How have you been?" he asked.

I shrugged my shoulders and replied, "So so."

The waitress came over and asked what he wanted.

"What are you having?" he asked me. I told him I was having an Irish coffee, which seemed appropriate for the cold, nasty weather. He asked the waitress to bring him a half cup of coffee and some whipped cream on the side, with the explanation, "I B-Y-O-B'ed."

"Huh?" the waitress said.

"Brought my own bottle," he said.

The waitress grumbled something under her breath and left the table.

"Boy, boy, boy," Bobby Jack said. "Am I tired."

"Is that a question or just a statement?" I asked.

"A statement," he answered. "That Belinda, she's something else."

"You should have brought her. She sounds like someone I'd like to meet." He had mentioned Belinda several times before.

He gave me his famous look of disdain and said, "And have her hang all over me while I'm trying to talk to a pal? No way."

As I previously stated, this is standard fare from Bobby Jack. He is of all men most predictable, which is not something I hold against the lad. There are advantages, even some comfort, in knowing there are some things on which you can depend.

I invited Bobby Jack to join the group on Sunday, and casually mentioned my house guest. When I told him the man called himself Jesus, he gave me a somewhat incredulous look but didn't start asking a lot of inane questions. Bobby Jack is pretty unflappable.

About that time the waitress returned with his half cup of coffee and whipped cream on the side. Bobby Jack opened his cooler, took out a red soda pop, opened it and poured a couple of jiggers in the coffee, stirred it and topped the beverage with whipped cream. The waitress looked on in surprised disgust, so I ordered another Irish coffee and hoped no one else had witnessed the drink Bobby Jack had mixed.

"What do you call that thing?" I asked.

"It's an African coffee," he said. "You ought to try one. They're pretty tasty."

"I'll pass. That red soda pop you drink is enough to choke a maggot."

"Really, it's not," he said. "I used to raise maggots and red soda pop was one of the things I had on their diet."

Bobby Jack's revelation that he had once raised maggots was news to me, something he had never told me before. Of course, I wanted to know why he had raised such critters.

"They make great fish bait," he said.

"I didn't know that."

"Oh, yeah. European larvae is great fish bait."

"I guess it was a pretty successful undertaking then."

"No, it was a dismal failure," he said. "Your American maggots just don't make as good a fish bait as European maggots."

His anti-American remark angered me momentarily, but then I realized Bobby Jack hadn't meant anything by his statement. He wasn't trying to bait me, and I don't know anyone who knows more about fishing than Bobby Jack. He's a member of U.S. Bass, Pro Bass, and Bass Anglers Sportsman's Society, which goes by the acronym BASS. He's a member of a lot of other fishing organizations, too, but I can't remember all of them.

Frankly, I think it's Bobby Jack's obsession with fishing that hurts his chances of getting a date with a woman, or of establishing anything on the order of a lasting relationship with someone of the female gender. His hands always smell fishy.

The waitress returned to our table and sarcastically asked Bobby Jack if he wanted another half cup of coffee with whipped cream on the side. He said he did, then she wrinkled her nose and asked, "What's that I smell?"

Bobby Jack put the palm of a hand close to her nose, causing her to cringe. "It's bass," he said. "I went fishing this morning and caught a limit. Smells pretty good, huh?"

"Ugh!" she exclaimed, then walked hurriedly away.

"What's wrong with her?" he asked.

"Most women don't like a man with fish smell on his hands," I said. It wasn't the first time I'd tried to explain this obvious fact to Bobby Jack, but he couldn't understand. He is a man who doesn't see anything wrong with a little honest fish smell on the hands. Still, I persisted, "Why don't you wash your hands after cleaning fish?"

"To me, there's nothing smells better than an old bass," he said. "Besides, what are you going to use to wash off the smell?"

"Boraxo Powdered Hand Soap works just fine." It is the same product I always recommend to Bobby

Jack when the subject of smelly hands comes up.

He grunted, "Maybe I'll try it," which is what he says every time.

Rather than become frustrated at Bobby Jack's ignorance on the subject of smelly hands, I changed the subject and started telling him about my encounter with the man who called himself Jesus. When I told him the man claimed to be the Son of God, he pondered the statement a few minutes and said, "I sort of doubt it."

"I hope to hell you don't think I believe it."

"Well, you are pretty gullible," he said.

I couldn't believe he said it. Not Bobby Jack. Not the world's most gullible human being, a man who sprays crawfish scent on a fishing lure and thinks it attracts bass from a mile away.

"Where do you get this gullible crap?" I asked.

"Don't get huffy," he said. "It's just that you don't know the Bible all that well and you might be deceived."

"I know a lot more Bible than I'm given credit for knowing," I challenged.

"I'm not going to argue with you," Bobby Jack said, "but if I meet the man on Sunday I can tell you right off if he's Jesus Christ or not."

"I can tell you right now that he isn't," I said, "but I'm curious as to how you think you can determine whether he's the real Jesus or not."

"I've got my ways."

About that time a booming voice rang out, "Hey

guys, sorry I'm late."

He of the good lungs was Bum Criswell, who is a polo coach for one of the more affluent private high schools in the area. At one time Bum was a football coach, but decided the game moved too slowly and offered no future. He gave some thought to coaching baseball, but after careful evaluation decided polo is the game of the future. He thinks polo is fast becoming the national pastime.

Arguing with Bum on this subject is somewhat akin to challenging the heavyweight boxing champion of the world to a few rounds. It's a no win situation. The man is totally committed to polo, even plans to write a series of books on the sport. He is forever writing letters to the sports editors of both newspapers, criticizing them for the lack of high school polo coverage.

Bum has attempted, unsuccessfully I might add, to start a worldwide Little League Polo program, with Dallas being the site for the World Series of Little League Polo. Bobo Harrison, who thinks Bum is a kook, primarily because Bum also wants to play center for our touch football team, says Bum could save himself a lot of trouble by just sending a trophy to the Taiwanese Little League Polo Team. Bobo's contention is that anything that is Little League will be won by Taiwan, since a team from that country always dominates the Little League Baseball World Series.

But Bum is not easily dissuaded. He's a visionary, a man who thinks Little League Polo is only the beginning, that it will eventually lead to Babe Ruth, Connie Mack and Stan Musial polo leagues.

I've tried to explain to Bum that not everyone can buy, house and feed a horse, but he says buying everyone in the country a horse would be cheaper than the mass transit plan proposed by the DART board. Of course, that's logic that can't really be disputed.

Still, I've tried to get across to Bum that it might be hard to get the citizenry of Dallas and other cities across the country to approve a sales tax to support polo. He simply asks, "Why not?" He claims sales tax goes for a lot of programs less deserving than polo, which is another unarguable point.

Bum's real plan, however, is to get his polo scheme funded by United Way. "If a person doesn't buy certain things, he or she doesn't have to pay sales tax," he says. "But there's no escaping United Way. Almost all employers pressure their employees to give to United Way."

Another of my arguments is that polo leagues shouldn't be named after Babe Ruth, Connie Mack and Stan Musial, all baseball people. Bum's rebuttal is that Babe, Connie and Stan would have been polo people if the opportunity had been there.

"Connie Mack was a great horseman," he says.

Again, it's something I can't dispute, since I know very little about Connie Mack's personal life. I just know he wore a double breasted suit, tie and fedora when managing his baseball team.

I had asked Bum to join us for drinks, and he wasn't late, though he had greeted us with an apology for tardiness. I had told him to meet us after polo practice.

"I didn't know you were coming," Bobby Jack said.

"And I didn't know you were going to be here," Bum said.

There was no animosity in the statement of either man, though neither could stand the other. However, their dislike for each other was something neither would admit. Bobby Jack considered it a duty to love everyone, and Bum thought it unsporting to dislike an adversary.

The waitress cautiously approached the table and asked Bum what he wanted. "I'll have one of those," he replied, pointing to my drink. I told her I'd have another, too.

"Do you want another of the same?" she asked Bobby Jack.

He nodded in the affirmative.

"What are you drinking?" Bum asked.

"African coffee."

"Good drink," Bum said, having absolutely no idea as to the ingredients of an African coffee.

"Would you like to have one?" Bobby Jack asked.

I hastened to reply, "Bum had better stick to the Irish coffee. African coffee and Irish coffee just don't mix."

"I think I can make my own decisions, Mark," Bum said. "That's a bad habit of yours, making decisions for other people."

"Sorry," I said. "Maybe an African coffee would be just the thing for you."

When the waitress returned with our drinks, Bobby Jack told her to bring Bum a set-up like his. Bum expressed his appreciation, then turned a little green around the gills when watching Bobby Jack mix his drink. He looked at me in dismay, and I looked away.

We talked for a while about nothing in particular, and I invited Bum to come over to the house on Sunday. He agreed to do so, asked if he could bring anything. I told him I'd appreciate it if he wouldn't bring something, that being the horse he usually rode over to the house and put in my backyard.

I could tell the request miffed him a bit, because Bum rides a horse practically everywhere. In fact, he had ridden a horse to the Harvey House and had tied the reins to a door of my car, another practice that annoys me.

He also wears a polo outfit everywhere, including the funny little hat. And because Bum is kind of short and fat, he looks a bit comical in the tall boots and riding pants.

Anyway, because he sulled like an opossum after me saying something about his horse, I told him to ride on over to the house and put his horse in the backyard. I have a good shovel, and if I didn't get around to cleaning up after the horse, so what? The yard probably needs fertilizing.

I'll have to give Bum credit. After flapping his mouth at me about the African coffee, he drank it. He grimaced as though he was downing a cup of castor oil, but he managed to polish it off. He even forced a weak grin and said, "That's good."

"Do you want another?" I asked.

He gave me one of those *I could kill you* looks and faintly replied, "One's enough."

Bum was born and raised in Dallas' exclusive Highland Park. And like the dutiful son of so much old Highland Park money, he went to Southern Methodist University. SMU, of course, did not have a polo team, which at the time was not a problem for Bum. It was much later in his life that he became obsessed with polo.

Though always chubby and built for comfort rather than athletic achievement, Bum aspired to greatness on the football field. He reached the pinnacle of his career as a senior when he was named fifth team quarterback, thanks to a million dollar grant from his father to the athletic department.

The million dollar endowment is in the name of *Bum Criswell: The Kid Who Wouldn't Give Up,* though Bum was not adverse to waving a white flag on the football field. The tenacity he now has for polo is something that has come with age. I'm sure it is only a matter of time before he devises plans for a Seniors Polo Circuit, similar to that of the Professional Golf Association.

If you're wondering how Bum ended up with the name Bum, it's a family name. It's my understanding that the name came from his mother's side of the family, something Bum's father affectionately called his brother-in-law, Bum's mother's brother.

Since Bobby Jack wanted to talk fishing and Bum wanted to talk polo, we ended up talking about the man who called himself Jesus. I certainly didn't suspect Bum of sending the man my way, because he was just too busy promoting polo. But I'd gone through the people with whom I associated most, and I still didn't have a clue as to who was behind the insideous plot to screw up my mind. I was ready to grasp for straws, for anything that would expose the plotters. I figured Bobby Jack or Bum might have heard something, might know something, but both claimed to be innocent of any knowledge regarding my plight.

I believed they were telling the truth, and the one thing I was sure of was that they weren't working together.

"Bobby Jack tells me he has a test for the man that will expose him for the fraud he is," I said.

"What is it?" Bum asked.

"Just be at Mark's house on Sunday and you'll see," Bobby Jack said.

We talked for quite a while, had far too much Irish and African coffee, then I went home. The man who called himself Jesus was there, and he had fixed a nice dinner for me. I had known him only a brief time, but he was always so thoughtful that I felt a bit guilty about talking behind his back. And maybe it was too much booze, but I was beginning to wonder, what if he's real?

During the meal I asked, "How was your day? Did you sell any hubcaps?"

"I sold one set to your friend Ribs," he said.

"Ribs?"

"Yes, he came by, bought the hubcaps and invited me to go coon hunting with him tomorrow night. He said something about asking you and Joe Don to go."

I chuckled. "Are you going?"

"I don't have any specific plans," he said. "I thought it might be enjoyable."

I laughed again.

"You find it amusing?"

"I find it funny," I said. "Jesus Christ on a coon hunt."

X

Ribs' Volkswagen was more than a little crowded. Ribs was driving, the man who called himself Jesus was sitting in the front passenger seat, and I was sharing the back seat with Joe Don and Blackie. The dog kept licking my face and, because of the crowded conditions, it was impossible to fight him off.

Knowing some of the things dogs will eat, I've never been one to enjoy the slurp of a dog's tongue. I've never understood people who kiss dogs. I don't think anyone would want to kiss a person they suspected of eating the things dogs will eat.

Of course, there are those who will say that I've kissed a lot of dogs in my time, referring to some of the females who have crossed my path. I figure those females got worse than I got, because I'm no prize.

I knew if I acted disgruntled about Blackie, Ribs would use my complaint as a springboard for one of his tirades on prejudice. He's a lot more vehement about prejudice against dogs than against people. He is specifically concerned about prejudice toward coon dogs, which he thinks represent the last great bastion of truth in our society. I'm not sure just why he thinks this, but am sure that I don't want to know.

"How far is it to this coon hunting place?" I asked.

"About sixty miles," Ribs answered. "We'll be there before you know it."

I didn't know if I could handle Blackie's halitosis for sixty miles, but thought his fetid breath might be better than what Joe Don was having to endure. Blackie's rear end kept bumping his face.

Ribs was ecstatic about all of us going coon hunting with him. I'm not sure why I had agreed to come along, but Joe Don was in the car because I had persuaded him it would be a fun way to spend a Saturday night. So far, his fun had been limited to viewing Blackie's rear end.

Things weren't great, but they were peaceful until Joe Don did what I should have known he would eventually do. He lit up a cigarette.

"Hey, man!" Ribs exclaimed. "That smoke's going to screw up Blackie's nose."

"From where I'm sitting, I didn't know he had a nose," Joe Don said.

I complained, "You're going to choke all of us to death, Joe Don. It's too cold to roll down a window."

He grunted, "I guess all of you think you'll get lung cancer if I smoke. What do you think about smoking, Jesus?"

"It's stupid."

The way he said it took all of us off guard, and

caused Ribs and me to laugh. Joe Don didn't laugh, but he didn't get mad, either. At least, I couldn't see any anger on what little of his face was visible behind Blackie's rear end. And he promptly put out his cigarette.

Never one to leave anything alone, I addressed a question to the man who called himself Jesus. "Why don't you tell us the difference between the Christian smoker and the Christian non-smoker?"

He sighed. "It's simply a difference of being stupid and smart."

One of my more irritating habits, or so I've been told, is that once I get on a subject I don't know when to quit. I get considerable enjoyment out of making others uncomfortable, and I knew any discussion on the evils of cigarette smoking would bother Joe Don. So, I said to the man who called himself Jesus, "I'd appreciate it if you'd be a little more specific about the difference in the Christian smoker and the Christian non-smoker."

I thought maybe I'd irritated him a bit, because there was a certain crispness to his voice when he said, "Mark, your only interest is in starting an argument, but I'll be glad to tell you what I think of cigarette smoking. Or for that matter, any kind of smoking."

"Right on," Ribs said. At times it's difficult to pinpoint the era from whence his conversation might come.

"Joe Don, I want you to know that what I say is

out of concern for you and not to appease Mark," the man who called himself Jesus said, "but it bothers me that people will abuse their bodies with cigarette smoke and then want to blame God for their health problems. But the cigarette smoker doesn't just abuse his or her own body, but also the health of everyone with whom they have contact."

"Right on," Ribs said again.

"This is no parable," the man continued, "but tell me, Joe Don, what would happen if you took four puffs off the tail pipe of this car while the motor was running?"

"I'd die of carbon monoxide poisoning," Joe Don replied.

"That's right, and it's something that every sane, informed person knows," the man said. "If you inhaled what the tail pipe is emitting, it would go into your system and convert to carboxy hemoglobin, which actually shuts off the oxygen supply to the heart muscle and vein wall, causes a brain problem and you die.

"Carbon monoxide is so bad that persons working in plants that produce it are restricted by government health standards to breathing no more than four hundred parts at any one time. That's the limit. But when you take a puff off a cigarette, you breathe in twenty-eight hundred to three thousand parts with every breath. Of course, you don't keep it all. You blow about half of it out on your friends, which means you over expose them, too."

Carboxy hemoglobin? Heart muscle and vein wall? Who was this guy anyway? Wasn't there anything he didn't know? Not that he was arrogant about his knowledge or anything like that. Actually, he spoke matter-of-factly, not patronizing in the least.

Joe Don argued, "A cigarette's not going to kill you, not like sucking in carbon monoxide from the tail pipe of a car."

"Just not as quickly," the man who called himself Jesus said. "Cigarette smoking over a period of time simply causes emphysema, lung cancer, stroke and heart disease. Smoking causes these diseases not only in the smoker, but also in those around him."

"Then cigarette smokers are murderers," I said, "and murderers can't enter the Kingdom of Heaven. Isn't that right?" I pride myself on being the master protagonist.

The man who called himself Jesus sighed. "I am salvation, the way, the truth and the life. Only through belief in me can anyone enter the Kingdom of Heaven."

The way he said it, the calmness and sincerity in his voice, stunned and shocked me. I have to believe it did the same to Ribs and Joe Don, though I couldn't read it in their faces. Granted, I couldn't see all of Joe Don's face. Blackie was still causing problems in that regard.

What I'd rapidly learned throughout the week,

though, was that this charlatan who posed as Jesus was dramatically affecting my friends. It was as though they were actually believing and accepting everything he said. It was hard for me to accept the fact that some of my friends were so gullible, that my intellect and comprehension level was so superior to theirs.

Why didn't this man affect me in the same way? What were my friends seeing, feeling and hearing that I couldn't see, feel and hear?

I tried to get back to the subject at hand with, "A couple I know are chain smokers and their baby has all sorts of respiratory problems."

"There are children in some lands who die of malnutrition," the man who called himself Jesus said, "but in this land of plenty many die and suffer because their parents refuse to give up harmful substances. And then they want to blame God for their suffering and the suffering of their children. As I've told you before, Mark, man makes his own choices."

My response was, "I heard about these people who were so angry because their son was killed in an automobile accident that they had SCREW GOD printed on some T-shirts and wore them to the kid's funeral."

"I don't have a T-shirt like that," Ribs said, quickly. He was wearing a CHITLIN POWER T-shirt.

The eyes of the man who called himself Jesus took on a weary look. "God gives man the freedom of choice, he abuses it, then blames God for his wrong choices. When the driver of an automobile tries to take a thirty-miles-per-hour curve at seventy-miles-per-hour, loses control of the car and is killed, is the choice he made God's fault?"

Ribs chimed in, "Of course not. A black man wouldn't be blaming God for something like that. It's these funny colored folks that blame God for something that stupid."

I contributed, "I don't know whether you've noticed, Ribs, but the guy you're agreeing with is one of those funny colored folks."

The man who called himself Jesus continued, "When man chooses to drink alcohol and drive, is killed, kills or injures someone in an accident, is that God's fault? Is God responsible for every irrational act of man? Is it God's fault that in this country seventy-five to eighty people are killed every day in alcohol related automobile accidents? Is it God's fault that in this country there are more than a thousand people permanently injured every day as the result of alcohol related automobile accidents?"

There was no excitement in this voice as he spouted off the questions, but I was fairly certain that I recognized a tinge of anger. And from what I knew of the New Testament Jesus, he could get pretty worked up over things. Not that I thought this guy was the Jesus of the Gospels or anything like that. But if he was going to play his part right, there wouldn't be anything wrong in getting mad.

"If you're going to get off on booze, you've got the right man in the car," Joe Don said. "Mark's a pretty big supporter of the liquor industry."

I protested, "I don't drink that much."

My three companions all gave me incredulous looks. Even Blackie's rear end couldn't hide Joe Don's look from me. And it may have just been my imagination, but I think even Blackie's face showed disbelief at my statement.

"C'mon," I continued. "You guys will have J.C. here believing I'm a drunkard."

The man who called himself Jesus said, "I know what you are."

There was a bit of hushed silence, except for the hum of the car's engine and Blackie's panting, which gave me a chance to regroup and think of ways to redirect the conversation. I began by asking Ribs how he liked his new hubcaps.

"You know how it is," he replied. "It's impossible to replace originals. I'd kind of gotten attached to the old hubcaps."

"Yeah, I know what you mean," I said. "My BMW hasn't driven the same since I replaced the hubcaps." I was lying, of course, because I'm pretty sure the hubcaps Chico sold me to replace the ones stolen were the ones that were stolen. But empathizing with Ribs might get the conversation back to where it should be, which would be discussion of something totally irrelevant.

"The hubcaps I got from Chico's store look pretty

original," Ribs said.

"I'll bet," was my reply. "That was your first sale, wasn't it, J.C.?"

"Not my first," he said. "I had sold a couple of paintings on black velvet before Ribs bought the hubcaps."

"Is Chico doing a pretty good business down on Harry Hines?" I asked.

Ribs answered, "I'll say. There must have been a hundred people there when I was at the store. Of course, most of them were just standing there listening to Jesus talk."

For some reason, Ribs' response made me nervous. But I came on with my usual bravado. "It sounds like a few people are interested in seeing and hearing your act."

"There are always a few people interested in the truth," the man who called himself Jesus said.

"I wouldn't think you'd draw too elite a crowd down on Harry Hines," I said.

He laughed, but there was meaning to it. It was not an expression of merriment. "Wouldn't you expect me to draw the poor, the prostitutes, people who live without much hope?"

He had me there, because the New Testament Jesus attracted people like that, if I was correctly remembering what I'd been taught in Sunday School and church. Of course, where I'd always gone to Sunday School and church had been neat, clean and sanitized, sort of like a good hospital. But the people in the church, most of whom were dressed in the latest fashion, always talked about how Jesus loved the poor and downtrodden. And we were always being asked to give our money so somebody could go talk to the poor. I didn't mind giving a little money so long as I didn't have to go talk to them.

"Well, did Chico have much business today?" I asked.

"We had a very brisk business," the man who called himself Jesus said. Then I swear his eyes sparkled when he continued with, "I even sold Chico's picture of Jesus on black velvet."

"Aren't you afraid someone will get the wrong impression of Jesus?" I asked.

"How someone perceives me with their eyes is not important," he answered. "It's how I'm perceived in the mind and heart."

There he went with that stuff again, claiming to be the real Jesus. I wanted to protest, but Ribs and Joe Don seemed perfectly content with his statement. Unless they were in on the plot against me, how could they have been so easily taken in, and so quickly?

Joe Don interrupted my thoughts with a question for Ribs. "Are we going to shoot these coons that Blackie trees?"

"What kind of question is that?" Ribs responded. "Sure, we're going to shoot the coons, and maybe we'll get lucky and shoot a 'possum, too. Then I'm going to cook the coon and 'possum, along with a batch of sweet taters, and have all my white folks friends over for dinner."

"Ugh, you can count me out," I said.

"Have you ever eaten any coon or 'possum?" Ribs asked.

"No, but neither animal sounds very appetizing. Of course, I don't like sweet potatoes, either."

"Lord help, you don't like sweet taters?" Ribs hooted. "That's a slap in the face to every black man who ever walked on the face of this earth. I sure wouldn't want my sister to marry someone who didn't like sweet taters. For that matter, I wouldn't want her marrying someone who didn't like coon and 'possum, either."

"You don't even have a sister," I said.

Ribs feigned hurt. "I was just trying to make a point."

"Well, I hope I can bring down a ferocious coon with my three fifty seven magnum," Joe Don said.

Ribs grunted. "The kind of coons you've been shooting with that big revolver, you won't have any trouble killing a furry little animal. I think I'd better do the shooting with my twenty-two rifle, though. We want some meat left on the bones."

"Hell, if I'd known I wasn't going to get to kill anything, I wouldn't have come," Joe Don complained.

"You probably wouldn't have come if you'd known we were going to bitch and moan about you smoking in the car," I said.

"Smoking's not that important to me," he said. "You act like I can't live without a cigarette. I could quit smoking any time I like."

"You have quit," the man who called himself Jesus told Joe Don. Blackie still had Joe Don's face covered up, but I could see the man's face, and he was serious. If he could get Joe Don to quit smoking, that would be as good a trick as turning my margarita into water.

"Like I said," Joe Don agreed, "I don't need cigarettes."

"You weren't really planning to cook coon, 'possum and sweet potatoes, were you?" I asked Ribs. He had this inclination to BS, and I'm not referring to a bachelor of science degree.

"Of course I'm going to cook 'em. Whether you realize it or not, I like something besides fried chicken, jalapeno blackeyed peas and cornbread."

"I didn't say you didn't," I responded.

"Well, that's all you ever serve at your house."

"I thought that was all you ever wanted."

"I like a little variety," Ribs said.

"Okay, so what do you want next Wednesday night?" I asked.

"What's Wednesday night?" Ribs asked.

I sighed. "I'm inviting you to dinner on Wednesday night. You and Blackie, too."

Ribs pondered for a moment, then replied, "I can't make plans that far in advance."

The conversation continued at an inane clip for

the remainder of the trip. We finally turned off the main highway and, for some time, traveled a dirt road back into the woods. Our stopping place was a cleared area that was obviously a wilderness campsite, in that there were no modern conveniences. Several pickups with campertops were parked in the area in helter-skelter fashion, and several campfires were going. Men and dogs were milling about.

I couldn't help but notice that we were the only hunters traveling in a Volkswagen. When we exited the little car, I jokingly told Joe Don that he had something brown on his nose. He didn't appreciate my humor, told me Blackie's rear end could ride on my face during the trip home.

While I had very little expertise in coon hunting (meaning none), the atmosphere was quite exciting and I was beginning to think it might be enjoyable. I couldn't help but note that I was the best-dressed of all the coon hunters in the camp. I had dropped by *Abercrombie and Fitch* and picked up a complete safari outfit.

Ribs had outfitted the man who called himself Jesus, though he was not exposing the T-shirt I was sure he had been provided. He was wearing what I guessed was old Army clothing, including the black boots. He had a REBEL LURES cap on his head.

Joe Don was wearing stuff that looked as though it had been stolen from the police SWAT team. And Ribs, except for the exposed T-shirt, was dressed like his interpretation of a lumber jack.

I'll say this for Ribs. He knows coon hunters and he knows coon hunter talk. He was the only black coon hunter in a group of about twenty or so men, so he was easily identifiable. I mention this only because everyone seemed to recognize and know him. Maybe it would have been a little different if there had been another black man in the group.

Ribs introduced us to all the men in the camp, but we ended up settling down around the fire of one Beep Jenkins, a man who had come down from Oklahoma to enjoy the camaraderie and the hunt. Beep poured us tin cups full of black coffee that was as thick as good syrup, but it's the kind of coffee you're supposed to drink on a coon hunt. The only problem I had with it were coffee grounds lodging between my teeth.

"You boys get you a plate there and have some vittles," Beep semi-commanded. "Sorry that we've already eaten up all the coon, but we've got some ham and red beans that'll put hair on your chest. About the ham, Jesus, I'm real sorry. I know you Jews don't eat pork."

The man who called himself Jesus sighed and said, "I don't mind eating ham."

"Oh, that's right, I don't guess you'd be orthodox, would you?" Beep said.

"I'm not . . . oh, never mind," the man replied.

I have to say that Beep's beans and ham were the best I've ever eaten, but maybe part of it had to do with the setting. Here we were in the wilderness, the cold north wind biting our exposed noses, and we were sopping the bean juice out of our tin plates with white bread, sitting around the fire on old logs that had been dragged up. Of course, Beep was sitting in a lawn chair, ready to hold court like the king of the hunt. The dogs were doing their part by walking around sniffing each other, then sniffing us to see if there was any difference in the smell.

It was Ribs who said, after a swig of coffee, "You know, it doesn't get any better than this." Ribs can be pretty profound, though I think I'd heard his statement somewhere before.

Out of the blue Beep said, "There's nothing quite like a cold nosed hound."

Everyone nodded agreement, except the man who called himself Jesus. I figured he didn't know that much about coon hunting. And though it was my first hunt, I was beginning to get a real feel for the sport.

It soon became obvious to me that all the coon hunters looked to Beep for direction, because before long they were all gathered around our fire. There was a lot of chewing, dipping, spitting, and crotch scratching, and a lot of bragging about various dogs. A couple of guys got in an argument about whether new Beechnut tobacco was moister or softer, but the highlight of the evening came when Beep gave his personal coon hunting testimony.

It all started when someone asked Beep what he would do if he had a million dollars. He straightened his wiry little body up in his chair, wiped some tobacco juice off a chin that had about a three-day growth of beard on it, and said, "I guess I'd just buy some more coon dogs."

There was sort of a rumble of appreciation that went through the gathering, all good men and true to their calling. They understood Beep and what he was saying.

Beep's thin red hair was beginning to gray up in spots, his face had more lines than a Dallas city map, there were sun spots on the crusty old skin, and his ears were more prominent than a donkey's. His PURINA FEEDS *gimme* cap was splotched with grease and sweat from days in the sun, his overalls were faded, his brogans scuffed, and his old brown coat was tattered and stained with coon blood and god knows what else. But in spite of it all, he was a princely man with a princely bearing.

Beep's poignant story was one that brought a tear to almost every eye, though I'll swear that I saw the man who called himself Jesus chuckle.

Beep had been an oil man and a banker, and during his early years he rarely ever came up with a dry hole. The money flowed as freely as the oil, so Beep became a millionaire several times over. He invested wisely, buying land and a few banks. "I always felt my strength," Beep said, "was in my love of the land and its people."

According to Beep, his one and most devastating weakness was in his choice of women. He had been married a half dozen times, all ending in divorce because of incompatibility. It was not that the women were incompatible with Beep, but with his coon dogs. Beep could tolerate a lot of things, but he would not tolerate a woman raising her voice at one of his dogs.

"A coon dog's psyche is a fragile thing," Beep said. "You let a woman start yelling at and bossing a coon dog around and the first thing you know the dog won't be worth a damn."

There was a chorus of "amens" when Beep said that.

Beep spit out the wad of chewing tobacco he had in his mouth, having sucked all the juice out of it, reached inside his Beechnut pouch and got another wad that he slowly placed inside his cheek. The man was a spellbinder, using every technique employed by a good speaker. He got the tobacco situated properly before continuing.

"Coon hunters," Beep said, "are what this great country is all about. Without the truth and logic of the coon hunter, there is no such thing as real freedom. The coon hunter has been the fiber that has kept America great through all its trials and tribulations."

Without going into excessive detail, Beep lost all his money to his six wives. But it was the last wife who really did him in, having had him committed to a mental institution for a short period of time. His saneness was questioned when he paid one million dollars for a champion coon dog, a purchase he called the wisest of all his investments.

"That champion dog is still with me, has sired hundreds of pups for me, most of which I've sold for five thousand dollars each," Beep said. "The woman's not with me, and there's not one damn thing she ever did for me that was worth five thousand dollars. Now you boys tell me, which is most valuable, a good coon dog or a woman?"

A rumble of appreciation for Beep's counsel went up from the gathering, and Ribs yelled out, "Right on."

To the man who called himself Jesus, Beep said, "You were wise not to marry."

I thought I caught the man rolling his eyes and giving a look of dismay, but I'm not sure. The only light we had was from the roaring campfire, and it's hard to read faces by campfire light. It's almost as hard as by dawn's early light. What startled me was a man as perceptive as Beep accepting the man who called himself Jesus for what he claimed to be, which was the real Jesus Christ.

But then Beep started saying some things I found offensive, and which I thought would make Ribs madder than a hornet.

"Coon hunting," he said, "is the way any man can lift himself above his environment. You take Ribs here, if he hadn't started coon hunting he might have ended up a shiftless black man on welfare, one who spent all his time either stealing or trying to steal something from a white man. But Ribs saw the light, bought himself a coon dog, and now he's one of the most respected men in Dallas. Now he can't be accused of spending his nights out robbing and raping white women, because he's putting his free time to good use by coon hunting. He has discovered the sport of kings."

The men cheered, spit, and Ribs looked a little sheepish. I think he blushed, but it's kind of hard to tell. It was obvious, though, that Beep's praise was something akin to receiving the *Congressional Medal of Honor.*

Beep added the clincher on Ribs' behalf when he said, "Some of you may not know it, but Ribs' dog Blackie is one of the sons of my million dollar coon dog, Oklahoma Crude."

The men cheered again, spit, scratched their crotches, and a fight broke out between the two arguing over whether new Beechnut was moister or softer. A bucket of water had to be thrown on them to break up the fight.

After order was restored, Beep said, "It's our custom at these Saturday night coon hunts to honor a hunter by naming him *Coon Hunter of the Week*. Tonight that honor goes to Ribs Davis, who continues what I modestly say has become a tradition. Every winner so far has bought a coon dog from me, all sons and daughters of Oklahoma Crude.

The men cheered, spit, scratched their crotches, and the two who had been fighting about whether new Beechnut was softer or moister hugged each other. It was a touching moment as Ribs took his place at Beep's side.

"We have another first," Beep said. "Ribs is the only black man ever to be named *Coon Hunter of the Week.*"

Again the men cheered, spit, scratched their crotches, and the two who had been hugging each other got in another fight. Another bucket of water was thrown on them to break it up. They were wet, muddy, and ice was forming on their clothing. They showed good judgment by getting close to the fire, showing coon hunters are intelligent. Then both got a chew of Beechnut out of the same pouch.

Beep continued his presentation, "Ribs, we have a few gifts for you. And gentlemen, I'd appreciate it if you'd hold your applause until I'm finished. First, we have a year's membership to the National Rifle Association, the only decent gun-loving organization in these United States. I'm proud to be on the NRA's state board of directors, and if you love America and coon hunting, I know you're a member. Ribs is already a member, so this gift will be a membership renewal. This membership renewal is courtesy of WBAP radio, the coon hunters station. And anybody who doesn't like country music and the Texas Rangers or Houston Astros baseball teams isn't welcome in this group."

The men couldn't control themselves. They applauded, spit, hit each other on the shoulders with their fists, did some more crotch scratching. Beep was on a roll.

"And the same goes for those who don't like the Dallas Cowboys or Houston Oilers," Beep yelled, provincially.

Again, applause, spitting, crotch scratching, emotions running rampant.

Beep calmed the men with an uplifted hand, then continued, "Ribs, we got a bumper sticker for you, but dadgumit, I hope you'll be getting rid of that Volkswagen and getting you a pickup real soon. It's not right for a dog with Blackie's bloodlines to be riding in a Volkswagen."

Ribs grinned and replied, "As soon as I get the note paid off on Blackie, I'm getting me a pickup."

The men cheered, spit, and pounded each other on the arms.

Then Ribs showed his new bumper sticker to the group and they cheered and started spitting again. The bumper sticker read: KILL A COMMIE.

"We have one more gift for you, Ribs, but you're not going to be able to use it right away," Beep said. "It's a gunrack for that new pickup you're going to buy."

The men cheered, spit, and stomped their feet. It was a time of great elation. A few men even started dancing a jig. Then they started yelling, "Speech, speech," wanting Ribs to acknowledge the honor just bestowed on him.

Ribs was all choked up and found words hard to

come by. The men understood, could relate to the tears that formed in his eyes. There was, after all, no greater honor than to be named *Coon Hunter of the Week.*

It would be nice to say that Ribs just choked out a few words of thanks and let it go at that, but it was not to be. Instead, he insisted on a musical thank you. I didn't even know he had put his accordion in the trunk of the car, but it's probably just as well. If I had known, I would have found an excuse for not going on the hunt.

Ribs mostly played country/western stuff, and the coon hunters seemed to have much more appreciation for his music than I did. A lot of them sang along, when they weren't spitting. A few hit high notes while they were scratching their crotches. Coon hunters and baseball players probably rank at the very top of the sports spectrum in terms of spitting and crotch scratching.

The man who called himself Jesus may have had the best line of the night when he said, "Now you know why we give angels harps, not accordions."

Joe Don kept asking, "When are we going to shoot a coon?"

It was late, and no one had shown any inclination to seek out a coon, but I said, "Relax. It must not be time to go after a coon. These guys are pros."

Frankly, I wasn't all that anxious to wander around in the woods at night, to fight my way through briar patches and brush. I was quite content to just sit around the campfire, drink coffee, and learn more about the sport. Joe Don's always been the impatient one.

It was a little surprising to learn that coon hunters as a whole are a bit opinionated, though I've never been one to label a group of people. The consensus was that the Redbone Hound is the finest of all coon dogs, primarily because those are the kind of dogs Beep raises.

"Your Bluetick, Redtick, English, Black and Tan, Plott and Walker are all good dogs," Beep generously conceded, "but a Redbone is by far the best dog money can buy."

Beep even had a definite idea about the type light a man should use for coon hunting.

"God meant for the hunter to use a carbide light or He wouldn't have given us carbide," Beep said.

I looked at the man who called himself Jesus, who just shrugged his shoulders and chuckled.

Beep continued, "A coon will look at a carbide light better than he will a battery light. The carbide light is not too bright and it's not too dim. It's just right."

Surely, Beep was giving his coon hunting seminar for our benefit. All of the other men knew this, had heard it before. I figured most of them, who nodded affirmatively at everything Beep said, just enjoyed being in the presence of greatness. It does give one a special feeling.

"I think modern, always have," Beep said.

"That's why I have an air-conditioned dog trailer. Before going to bed for the night, a man ought to see that his dogs are fed and watered."

I seem to recall something like that in a western movie, but it had to do with a man's horse.

"You ever use a mule for coon hunting?" someone asked Beep.

"Of course, I've used mules," Beep answered, the tone of his voice making the questioner's question seem ridiculous. "Up around Wichita Falls, just about everybody who hunts coons rides a mule. This country's just not conducive to mule riding. A friend of mine up in Oklahoma even has a mule that will tree coons."

"Why don't you bring him down here sometime," a listener suggested.

"Can't," Beep said. "Can't get that ol' mule across the Red River."

"Why's that?" someone said.

"Anytime he gets close to water he goes crazy," Beep explained. "The mule likes to fish better than he likes to hunt."

I almost laughed, but quickly noted that everyone else was taking Beep's story seriously. To these men, what Beep said, no matter how outlandish, was gospel truth.

It was a little after ten o'clock when the hunt finally began. One of Ribs' benefits as Coon Hunter of the Week was to hunt with Beep Jenkins and Oklahoma Crude. Those of us who had come to hunt with Ribs were allowed to tag along.

We weren't in the woods more than five minutes when the dogs picked up a trail and started barking. Beep said it was Oklahoma Crude who first barked on the trail and Ribs agreed. I couldn't tell the difference in the voices of the dogs, but it's something coon hunters know.

After about three or four minutes of frantic barking, all was quiet. It was quiet for maybe two or three minutes, prompting Joe Don to say, "I guess they lost the coon's trail."

Beep kind of chuckled at Joe Don's observation, but didn't say anything until the dogs started barking again, which was maybe another minute or so. "Oklahoma Crude and Blackie are so well trained," he said, "that they don't bark when they're crossing posted land."

Finally, after several minutes of constant barking, Beep and Ribs looked at each other by carbide light and the old hunter said, "They're treed."

For what seemed like an eternity, we battled our way through thickets and briars toward the barking dogs. By the time we arrived at the tree where Oklahoma Crude and Blackie were barking, I was as winded as if I had run five miles. That's merely speculation, of course, since I have never run five miles.

With their carbide lights, Beep and Ribs searched the tree for the coon the dogs were sure was there. Joe Don stood anxiously by with his three fifty seven magnum at the ready position. But nowhere could the hair of a coon be seen.

"There's no coon up there," Joe Don complained.

"The dogs must have beat the coon to the tree," Beep explained.

In the dim light, I looked at the man who called himself Jesus and he observed my gaze. Then he said for my benefit only, "You'd expect me to be on the coon's side, wouldn't you?"

The dogs treed twice more before we went back to camp, but we didn't see a coon. Joe Don was more than a little perturbed. But I couldn't help but notice that he hadn't smoked a cigarette during the entire evening. And he didn't smoke, or attempt to, during the drive home. I might not have objected if he had smoked in the car, because I had ample opportunity to get acquainted with Blackie's rear end.

XI

I was awakened by someone gently shaking my shoulder, or was I dreaming? For me, the world was not in focus. Even through a drawn curtain, I could tell there wasn't anything outside the window except darkness.

"Wake up," a voice said. "Breakfast is ready."

My mind does not work like a computer. It's more like an old vintage Royal typewriter, one with worn keys and irreplaceable parts. But when I finally got one of the keys unstuck, I recognized the voice as being that of the man who called himself Jesus. I groaned and rolled to the other side of the bed. He laughed.

"C'mon, Lazybones," he chided. "You asked me to wake you at six."

He was telling the truth. I had made such a request, but it was at a time when I was not in complete control of my faculties. If memory hasn't failed me, my request was made in the early morning hours en route home from the coon hunt, and seconds after Blackie had gassed me.

"C'mon," the man said again. "I made grits for breakfast."

His words were like magic, and I was suddenly

ready to believe he was anyone he chose to be. Grits affect me like that. The very sound of the word makes me want to start singing *Dixie* and I get chill bumps all over.

Had there not been a shortage of grits in the South during the Civil War, the Confederacy would not have allowed the North to think they had won. When you cut a southerner's grits ration, you get a listless individual who wants to do nothing but sit on the bank of a river and fish for catfish.

So, after the man who called himself Jesus told me he had fixed grits for breakfast, I robed and houseshoed myself and staggered to the breakfast table.

"Do you want anything with your grits?" he asked.

I gave him a look of dismay and he said, "I didn't think so."

After a generous helping of grits and a couple of cups of coffee, my voice came back to me and I thanked him for his kindness. Actually, I needed to get up early to get the spareribs on, because slow cooking is the key to great ribs. I cook them for several hours in the oven, drain the grease off, apply barbecue sauce liberally, then cook them some more. The meat is so tender it falls off the bone. Of course, you want to start with good ribs.

"You're obviously a connoisseur of grits," my guest said.

"True," I agreed. "I guess you read my *Texas*

Monthly article on *The Greatest Grits Restaurants in Texas.*"

"No, I didn't read it," he replied. "Of course I knew about it, but I didn't think it was that important."

His response made me even more certain he wasn't who he pretended to be. If I've read my Bible correctly, it was grits that God provided to the Children of Israel when they were wandering in the wilderness. I think God keeps a close check on the grits crop and on those who eat grits.

But the man who called himself Jesus shook his head in amazement and said, "I can't believe what you're thinking. You give God so little credit."

"What do you mean?" I asked. "I give God a lot of credit."

"You give Him credit for caring about things that don't matter," the man said, "which means you don't give Him any credit."

I didn't understand what the guy was talking about, but I'm not one to argue, especially on Sunday. Besides, I had to get the ribs in the oven, and I had to start psyching myself up for the Cowboys game and one of the most important touch football games we would play during the entire season.

"Hey, I hope we can count on you to play for us this afternoon," I said. "We're going to need some depth to beat the bunch we play today."

He laughed. "I don't care anything about football."

"That's un-American," I said, sourly. "More important, it's un-Texan."

"Okay, I'll play," he said.

It's what I wanted to hear. I still didn't believe he was who he claimed to be, but if he was it would give us a real edge over our opponents. I don't know why, but he gave me a look of resignation, as though he could read my mind.

"I guess you're going to church, aren't you?" I asked.

"Yes, that is my intention."

"I'd appreciate it if you'd grab an early service, because we're going to start our game at one."

"Well, I certainly wouldn't want church to mess up something as important as a touch football game," he said, sarcastically.

"This is not just another touch football game," I said. "It's one we've been pointing to for the past several weeks. These guys annihilated us early in the season."

He again shook his head in that "I give up" manner, which didn't bother me a bit. I just got me another cup of coffee, prepared the ribs and stuck them in the oven while he was reading the Sunday paper. I decided if he was who he claimed to be, he wouldn't have to read the paper. He would already know all the stuff in it.

"Anything of interest in the paper?" I asked.

"I was just reading here where Texas has a problem with overcrowded prisons and planned to put some inmates in a National Guard barracks in West Texas," he replied.

"That sounds like a good idea."

"Evidently not," he said. "A federal judge has ruled that it can't be done. The barracks are fine for National Guard troops, but not nice enough for prisoners."

If he was trying to get me stirred up, he had pushed the right button. I'm not one of those persons who thinks a prison ought to be like a country club.

"From what this judge says," he continued, "people can commit crimes without fear because he won't permit them to be placed in an overcrowded prison. And he's not going to allow them to be placed in inferior housing, either."

"Like the National Guard barracks?"

"That's right, like the National Guard barracks."

I slurred, "Brother. That's disgusting. Has the line changed on the Cowboys game today?"

He gave me that incredulous look and said, "I'm glad you keep your mind on things that matter."

"Hey, if you were from Dallas, you'd know that the Cowboys game is the only thing that does matter. We're talking serious time of the year here."

Maybe I am a wee bit provincial, but no one can shame me about it. I have two bumper stickers on my car. One reads KVIL LOVES TEXAS and the other, LOVE NEW YORK? TAKE I-30 EAST. Where

Texas is concerned, I'm a love it or leave it person.

During the first week the man who called himself Jesus stayed at my house, I noticed there were times when he didn't seem to pay too much attention to what I said, as though what I said wasn't all that important. He always acted, though, like he knew what I was thinking. It bugged me somewhat, but like all things it passed.

"Where are you going to church today?" I asked.

"We're having services at Chico's place," he replied.

"You're kidding?"

"No, I'm not kidding. Why would you think I'm kidding?"

"Well, I don't exactly think of church as being a place where I'm surrounded by old hubcaps," I said.

My response obviously annoyed him. "That's one of your problems," he said. "You're one of those people who equates stained glass, high ceilings and organ music with holiness and worship of God. The true believer can worship anywhere, under any conditions."

I shrugged my shoulders. "Okay, but what kind of people are going to worship at Chico's place?"

"The same kind of people who worship at the most elaborate church buildings in the city. People who need God."

"You know what I mean."

"I know exactly what you mean," he said. "You're talking about people who don't dress as well as you do, who don't drive BMWs, who don't live in nice houses, and who don't have respected professions."

I crawfished, "I wouldn't put it exactly like that."

"How would you put it?"

As I stated previously, I'm not one to argue, especially on the Lord's Day. "I'm concerned about the Eagles. I think they're really going to be primed for the Cowboys."

He sighed, straightened the newspaper, and left the room. He was dressed in an old robe I had given him and a bad case of five o'clock shadow clouded his face, so I figured he needed to go shave, shower and get ready for church. It never entered my mind that he left the room because he was teed off at me. I certainly felt no animosity toward him for his inability to understand the modern church and contemporary Christians. The man seemed intelligent enough, but there seemed to a lot that he didn't comprehend.

Another reason I doubted his authenticity was that he didn't have a beard. It's my feeling that the real Jesus wouldn't give up his beard, no matter what century he happened to be roaming the earth. I also figured him for a robe and sandal man, no matter what the style chosen by the majority of mankind. But this guy's clothes were not unique or stylish in any way. His suits and ties could have come off a Salvation Army truck.

Well, I was really too tired to worry about who he was, or about who had sent him my way. The coon hunt had been an enjoyable experience, except for having to ride with Blackie, but it had wiped me out. If I was going to be ready for the game, I needed some rest. So, I laid down on the couch in order to rest my eyes, with the grits I had eaten weighing heavily upon my stomach.

The next thing I remember was the doorbell ringing. I glanced at the clock on the fireplace mantle and saw that it was almost eleven o'clock. Though startled by the time, I didn't exactly spring from the couch. I did groan, get to my feet and houseshoed my way to the front door. It was Mary Lou.

"You look awful," she said. "I thought I'd come early and help you get dinner ready."

Mary Lou can be helpful, but she can also be a pain. She can be a special pain in the kitchen, where she is as helpful as mold on a loaf of bread. Cooking is not Mary Lou's thing. I can't even trust her to properly wash the lettuce for the salad.

I grunted, "Come on in. Do you want a cup of coffee?"

"I'd prefer a wine cooler."

"There's one in the refrigerator. Just make yourself at home while I shower."

"Where's the guy who claims to be Jesus?" she asked.

"He went to church, but he'll probably be home

pretty soon. Help yourself to a cooler and watch the tube while I shower."

The rivulets of water cascading off my head helped, but didn't wash all the cobwebs from my mind. The mental processes were in disarray, which some persons think is a permanent condition with me. However, I knew I would be mentally ready for both our game and the Cowboys game later in the afternoon. My mental dexterity was critical if we were to have any chance against the animals who were our opponents.

Proper dress is critical for touch football and for watching Dallas Cowboys football. I selected my mesh green and gold BAYLOR shirt with bear claws on the shoulders, green sweat pants, white socks with gold trim, and white Nike running shoes. I was ready.

Mary Lou was obviously not impressed with my dress. She laughed and said my outfit clashed.

"With what?" I asked.

"With everything," she said.

I wanted to say something derogatory about Mary Lou's dress, but it's hard to do. She dresses well and likes to show off her legs, which are about as good as any you will ever see. She has the legs to do pantyhose commercials.

On this particular occasion, though the temperature outside was in the low fifties, she was wearing shorts and a sweater top. Like I said, she likes to show off her legs, and they are always tan, thanks to the advent of tanning salons.

There is, however, one area about which Mary Lou is extremely sensitive. Though in her thirties, she still suffers from an occasional attack of teenage acne. By keen observation, I was fortunate enough to be able to detect a small blemish on her chin, which I joyously called to her attention. She scurried away to the bathroom to try to cover it with makeup, giving me great satisfaction and the assurance that she would not again, on this particular day, make fun of the way I was dressed.

Sue Beth was the next to arrive, and she had brought her fiance, Chigger Dodgen, with her.

"You look awful," she told me.

"Maybe you don't like green and gold," I said, "but these happen to be my alma mater's colors and . . ."

"I'm not talking about your clothes," she explained. "I'm talking about your eyes. They're bloodshot."

"Well, I went coon hunting last night."

Chigger spoke up, "If I had known, I would have gone with you. There's nothing I like better than a good coon hunt."

"Sugar, I don't think he's talking about the same kind of coon hunting you do over in Louisiana," Sue Beth said.

Chigger looked a bit baffled, but I'm used to folks looking that way. "I didn't think you were going to be able to make it to our little get-together," I said to Chigger. "I heard you were going to be picking up aluminum cans with your kids."

Chigger grunted. "That was the plan, but things just didn't work out. There are a few logistics problems when you have to coordinate things with twelve ex-wives."

I sympathized with Chigger's plight, though I couldn't honestly say I understood such logistics problems. I doubt that the Pentagon could have understood and handled his problem.

To give you an idea about Chigger's height, when he is standing next to Sue Beth the top of his head is about even with her bust line, and that's with his jockey hat on. He always wears his jockey hat, or at least he always has when I've been around him. Sometimes he even wears his goggles, though most of the time they're cocked up on the front of his hat.

One of my many suspicions about Chigger is that he's bald, though I can't prove it. I just know that some people are sensitive about baldness, and Chigger has always impressed me as being a very sensitive person.

Though Chigger wears his jockey hat and goggles, he sort of downplays being a jockey. He's not like a golfer or someone who has just learned to fly a plane. That is, he doesn't want to talk about it all the time. Sue Beth says his parents don't even know he's a jockey, them being Baptists and all. He has kept his profession a secret from them because such knowledge would break their hearts. They think he is a brain surgeon in Shreveport.

Chigger says he doesn't mind his folks knowing anything and everything about him, except that he has danced on occasion and that he is involved in a sport that depends on parimutuel wagering. "That would kill them," he says.

Except for the hat and goggles, Chigger never wears his jockey togs anywhere other than at the track. His non-professional attire includes reptile cowboy boots, Wrangler Jeans, a rattlesnake belt with a saucer-size Jack Daniels belt buckle, double-breasted cowboy shirts like the ones Wild Bill Elliott wore, and in winter a sheepskin coat. Chigger attaches special sentiment to the coat, because it was made from the pet sheep he had as a boy.

"I'm glad you could come," I told Chigger, "because we're going to need all the help we can get for today's game."

"You can count on me," he said, "just as long as I can be sure that no one will tell my folks I played football on Sunday."

I assured Chigger that his secret would be safe, that no one on either team would squeal on him. Of course, I couldn't be sure about our opponents, because they are guys who hit below the belt. But given the fact that Chigger's folks live back in a Louisiana swamp where the only means of transportation is a pirogue, I didn't figure word would get to them about our touch football game. However, with

the competition between Dallas teevee sportscast-
ers, there was a possibility that Chigger's involve-
ment in the Sunday fracas might be beamed into
the Pelican State.

I was willing to take the gamble.

"Anything to eat?" Sue Beth asked.

"Lots of chips, dips and junk like that," I answered. "There's even some leftover grits."

"Grits," she squealed. "Lead me to them."

Sue Beth's exclamation brought Mary Lou back
into the room to greet her pal. I greeted Mary Lou
with, "I see you got rid of that pimple."

She responded with a few well-chosen expletives,
plus some questions about heredity. I can't remember exactly what she said, since she was in an irrational state. Pimples do that to Mary Lou.

Anyway, Sue Beth found what was left of the
grits and devoured them. Then she started on the
chips, bean dip, cheese dip, and anything else that
would stay still long enough for her to get a chip in
it. Chigger watched admiringly, but didn't eat anything. He said he had to watch his weight.

When I heard a horse neigh in the back yard and
knew Bum Criswell had arrived. I opened the door
to the patio and let him in, watched with a degree of
fascination as his horse fertilized a portion of my
yard.

"Sorry, I'm late," he said, apologetically.

"You're not late," I said. "You're never late, but
you always apologize for being late."

I obviously ruffled his feathers, because his response was haughty. "Well, excuse me. By the way, you look horrible."

"Someone who wears a polo outfit to play football in shouldn't comment on another person's clothes."

"I'm not talking about your clothes," he said. "Your eyes are bloodshot."

"So I've been told."

Bum joined the others in the den and immediately got in a discussion with Chigger about horses. Chigger had a little difficulty understanding Bum's plan 'for Babe Ruth, Connie Mack and Stan Musial polo leagues, but was quite interested in helping provide horses for the ventures. I could see the dollar signs clicking in Chigger's mind as he computed his take for getting rid of some of the nags at Louisiana Downs.

"How are you and Sue Beth doing in acquiring land for a track?" I asked.

Chigger deferred to Sue Beth, who cleared her mouth long enough to say, "We've got options on some pretty good property around SMU."

"I don't understand why you insist on having a track in Highland Park," I said.

"You wouldn't understand," Bum said. "Sue Beth wants a track that has some class."

People who live in Highland Park think it is the most exclusive area in or around Dallas. And they have done a good job of convincing others. That's why an old frame, roach-infested house in the area sells for hundreds of thousands of dollars. The wealthy tear down nice houses in Highland Park and build bigger ones because doing so impresses their friends. It's the land that's expensive in the area because there's just not any left.

Many people in Highland Park have never been outside its boundaries. They think everything of value is inside its city limits. They have not heard about integration, which is another reason for Highland Park's popularity. They only know that the help comes in on the buses in the morning and leaves on the buses in the afternoon. And the Highland Park Police keep a close watch on the buses. They think blacks have their place, which is in South Dallas or playing ball for the Cowboys, Mavericks or Rangers.

There are a lot of women in the Dallas area who would trade their husband's testicles for a chance to live in Highland Park. It is the promised land of Yuppies.

"Does the Highland Park City Council know you're planning a track for the city?" I asked.

"Well, no," Sue Beth replied, "but I think they will be agreeable."

"You've got as much chance of getting their consent as anyone would have in getting the membership of the First Baptist Church of Dallas to vote for parimutuel betting," I said.

Bum grumbled, "You're such a spoil sport, Mark.

I've found the administration at SMU very agreeable to a polo team for the school."

"That's a little different."

"Maybe so," he agreed, "but you have a bad habit of shooting down a person's dreams. You don't have to be the devil's advocate in everything."

"Well, thank you very much. I guess I wasn't thinking, but another Louisiana Downs in Highland Park seems unrealistic to me."

"Small people have small dreams," contributed Chigger.

"You should know," I said.

What could have turned into a real argument was stymied when the doorbell rang. It was Jimmy Joe Johnson, resplendent in a designer jogging outfit, cowboy boots and cowboy hat. "You look awful" was the first thing he said to me.

"The outfit you're wearing doesn't look all that great," was my reply.

"I'm not talking about your outfit. I'm talking about your eyes," he said. "They're bloodshot."

Draped on one of Jimmy Joe's arms was Bumps Ann Grinds, who always looked like a model for *Frederick's of Hollywood.* Actually, she buys most of her stuff from *Fred's of Frisco,* a little town north of Dallas where she grew up and still lives. Bumps is about as sultry a dish as you would ever want to see. She has natural blonde hair with black roots and is one of Mary Kay Cosmetic's best customers.

As always, she insisted on giving me a kiss,

which cosmeticatized an entire side of my face. Her kiss caused my head to tilt at a dangerous angle, until I finally went to the bathroom and washed the makeup off.

Of course, Mary Lou is not one of Bumps' fans, which always makes for some interesting conversation when the group gets together. What makes things even more interesting is that Bumps likes Mary Lou, never really catches on to Mary Lou's sarcasm.

"Bumps," I said, "Mary Lou is having a little problem with acne. I'm sure she would appreciate it if you would tell her how you keep your skin so nice."

Mary Lou's "killer eyes" nailed me, but Bumps was already into a discourse on proper facial care, which basically consisted of just covering everything up with makeup.

Billy Bob was next to arrive and he began with what had become a familiar greeting. "You look awful."

"I went coon hunting last night, which is why my eyes are bloodshot."

"I'm not talking about your eyes," he said. "It's that outfit. But now that you mention it, green and gold just doesn't go with red."

"Don't you care about the school colors?" I asked. "Doesn't green and gold, *That Good Old Baylor Line,* mean anything to you?"

"No."

There are times when I think Billy Bob is too blunt, though most of the time he engages in long discourses to explain his position. Many judges wish he would be blunter, because they don't like Billy Bob. They don't understand him as I do.

"I really don't understand you," I said. "Everything you are, everything you've achieved in life, is a result of being educated at Baylor University."

He signed, "I know."

I checked on my other guests and found Sue Beth had created a shortage of chips and dips. Fortunately, I was aware of her capabilities in that regard, so I had laid in store a huge supply of Frito-Lay products, along with gallon containers of dip. Mentally, I likened myself to the Biblical Joseph, who was put in charge of supplies for Egypt. Fat chance of a Jew being put in charge of Egypt's food supply in this day and time.

Lately, since the man who called himself Jesus had been my house guest, a lot of Biblical thought had been transgressing in my mind. I've always been more religious than credited with being. Though never one to flaunt my knowledge of the scriptures, I do consider myself the equal to any man in religious thought when I put my mind to it.

"What's a three letter word for divine being?" The question was from Chigger, who was busy with a crossword puzzle in the newspaper.

"I don't know," I replied.

Bum was in serious discussion with Jimmy Joe

concerning his proposed polo leagues, asking Jimmy Joe to consider selling polo franchises instead of oil deals. "People are tired of oil," Bum said.

"I don't know," Jimmy Joe said. "I hate to deal in something speculative."

Billy Bob asked Bum what he knew about the Mideastern Polo League where camels, not horses, were used for the sport.

"Where is the Mideast?" Bumps asked. "Is that the New Jersey area?"

Jimmy Joe, obviously embarrassed by his girl friend's ignorance, gave her a look of disdain. "My gosh, Bumps, you should know the Mideast is somewhere around Philadelphia."

"Where's Philadelphia?" Bumps asked.

Jimmy Joe looked at me for help, but I wasn't giving any. I was building a frozen margarita and didn't want to get into an argument, especially on Sunday.

Chigger looked up from the crossword puzzle and said, "Philadelphia's here today. They're playing the Cowboys."

"I knew that," Jimmy Joe said.

"The Mideast Billy Bob is talking about is like Israel," Bum said.

"It can't be Israel," I said. "It's against Jewish religion to ride a camel."

"Where in the hell did you get that from?" Bum asked.

"It's in the Bible," I said.

"Well, I sure never heard that. Where is it in the Bible?"

"It's in the Book of Solomon," I said, "Chapter Twenty, Verse Six." I was bluffing as to the exact location of the information, but did remember reading something about Jews and camels.

"Do you have a Bible around here?" Mary Lou asked.

"I loaned my Bible to a friend," I said.

"How convenient," she said.

"Have you ever eaten any camel fries?" Sue Beth asked between bites of chips and dip.

"Are camel fries like calf fries?" Billy Bob asked.

"I think so," Sue Beth said. "They're little round things."

"Where in the world did you have camel fries?" Mary Lou asked.

"I had them a couple of years ago when I took that boat trip up the Nile."

"Is that in Ohio?" Bumps asked.

"Well, I can tell you this," I said. "Eating camel fries is a sin. The Old Testament specifically forbids people to eat the balls of any animal."

Sue Beth pondered, then responded, "I didn't know that."

"I didn't know fries were made of animal balls," Bumps said.

Jimmy Joe explained, "Not all fries are, Bumps. The fries we usually have are made from potatoes."

"You'd have to use really long polo sticks," Bum said.

"What are you talking about?" Mary Lou asked.

"I'm talking about playing polo on camelback," he answered.

"I sure wish we had a Bible here," Mary Lou said. "I'd like for Mark to show us where it says it's a sin to eat animal balls."

"I wish I had my Bible here, too, because I could sure as heck show you, Mary Lou."

"I'll be glad when that guy who calls himself Jesus gets here," she said. "Maybe he can tell us if you're lying."

"You're always trying to catch me in a lie," Mary Lou, "but you never have and you never will."

"Ha! I'd be more surprised if I could catch you telling the truth."

The doorbell interrupted the conversation. I answered and found Bobo standing there, beer can in hand. "I'm empty," he said.

"There's plenty of beer in the refrigerator."

"I like your outfit," he complimented. "The green and gold goes good with your red eyes."

Bobo got himself a couple of cans of brew and sat down on the couch next to Chigger. It was quite a contrast.

"Do you know a three letter word for divine being?" Chigger asked Bobo.

"Try T-O-M," Bobo suggested.

"Why Tom?" I asked.

Bobo shrugged his shoulders. "Tom Landry."

"It works," Chigger said.

"How have you been doing, Mary Lou?" Bobo asked. He has always been fascinated with her, can't understand why she and I can't get along.

"I've been doing fine," was Mary Lou's response. "I've been checking your column from time to time. It's nice to see that someone is finally championing the Snail Darter."

Bobo shrugged his shoulders again. "Someone has to take up for the little critters."

"When are we going to eat?" Sue Beth asked.

"We're going to eat during the Cowboys game," I said.

"When's the kickoff?" she asked.

"Three o'clock."

"If I have to wait until three o'clock to eat, I'll die."

"Our touch game starts at one," I said. "We don't want to eat until it's over. But I don't want you to starve, so I do have a bucket of chicken in the refrigerator that you can munch on until we start our serious eating."

"Hallelujah!"

I laughed. "I figured you'd approve."

"You are a darling," she said.

"Has anyone ever had chicken fries?" Bumps asked.

Everyone ignored her question, and I got busy and built myself another margarita. I had just completed it when Joe Don arrived. "That stuff's going to kill you," he said.

"Yeah, and smoking's going to kill you."

"I don't smoke."

"Since when?"

"Since last night."

"Well, bully for you."

"I'm serious, Mark, you ought to get off the sauce."

Ribs, Chico, Beep Jenkins and the man who called himself Jesus all arrived at the same time. Beep had decided to spend the night outside Ribs' apartment. Ribs had told Beep that he could have the bed and he would take the couch, but Beep said he would feel more comfortable sleeping in his camper with the dogs. In addition to Oklahoma Crude, Beep had brought eleven other dogs down for the hunt.

"I hope you don't mind," Beep said to me, "but I put all the dogs out in your backyard. They need to stretch their legs."

"I don't mind," I lied. "I just hope none of them get kicked in the head by a horse."

"Huh? You got a horse out there."

"Yeah, it's Bum Criswell's polo horse."

"I just hope the dogs don't eat him," Beep said.

Alarmed, I asked, "What do you mean?"

Beep explained, "Well, I had a couple of burros and the dogs ate them. Of course, a burro's not much bigger than an old rogue coon."

"Bum's horse is pretty big," I said.

"I doubt that they'd eat all of him then. I fed them this morning."

Beep was still wearing the same clothes he had on at the coon hunt, causing me to suspicion that he had slept in them. It was hard to tell, because they had looked slept in when I had first seen them. And Beep still hadn't bothered to shave.

It took a while to introduce Beep and the man who called himself Jesus to those in the group who hadn't met one or both of them. What surprised me was that everyone seemed so awed by the man who called himself Jesus. I was more awed by Beep.

"This is quite a coincidence, all of you arriving at the same time," I said to Ribs.

"Not really," he said. "We were all down at Chico's place listening to Jesus teach."

I was somewhat surprised. "Beep went down there? What did he think?"

Beep replied, "I can answer that for myself. Jesus makes a lot of sense. He's got the makings of a fine coon hunter."

"Well, it looks like you're developing a following," I said to the man who called himself Jesus.

"Believe it or not, I've had a pretty good following for quite a few years," was his reply.

"I'm not much of a church goer," Beep admitted, "but I'd be more regular if I could go to something like we had today."

I responded sarcastically. "Being in among all

those used hubcaps has to give one a sense of reverence."

Beep answered as though my comment had been serious. "No, it was more than the hubcaps. There was some real spiritual movement there today. You could feel it."

"Beep led the singing," Ribs said.

Beep added, "If I do have to say so myself, I'm a pretty fair country singer, have been for a lot of years. But Ribs did a good job of accompanying me."

"Ribs played the accordion?"

"That he did," Beep said, "and his music was like it came right out of Heaven."

I laughed. "I believe I would have preferred a capella."

"If we had wanted a capella, we could have gone to the Church of Christ," the man who called himself Jesus said.

I replied, "That brings up a point. With what denomination is this CHURCH AMONG THE HUBCAPS going to affiliate?"

"Why do you think it necessary for us to affiliate with any group?" the man said. "I told you before that denominations are man's idea, not God's."

I argued, "If you're not part of a denomination, you can't go to a convention. You won't have any Sunday School literature. You won't have a heirarchy to make decisions for you. You won't have colleges and seminaries. You won't have a mission board to send out missionaries for you. You won't have a theological doctrine to represent. You won't get much press. You won't even have a denominational newspaper. And you won't have any missionaries to come show slides to you about their work. More important, if you lose the church, it might be hard to get another one."

The man who called himself Jesus guffawed. "I'm glad you have such an insightful concept as to what the church is and ought to be. Is there anything else you'd like to add?"

He was teasing me and I knew it, but someone had to set the guy straight on the contemporary church. "Well, I would at least hope that you're going to get the CHURCH AMONG THE HUBCAPS to take up a collection to send you to the Holy Land. Without a trip to the Holy Land and some slides, you're doomed to failure."

He laughed again, then said in all seriousness, "There's no such thing as a specific Holy Land. Wherever God's Spirit is, that is the Holy Land."

I continued my argument with, "People tell me they go over to places like the Mount of Olives and get a special feeling about the presence of God."

"There's nothing wrong with that," he said, "but if a person has to go to a specific place to experience and feel the presence of God, then he or she needs to examine their relationship with God. A person should have just as strong a feeling of God's presence in a supermarket as on the Mount of Olives."

Bobo interrupted the conversation's flow with

the question, "Is the CHURCH AMONG THE HUBCAPS going to get into a softball league? I'd be interested in joining if you're going to have a softball team."

"Before you get a softball team started, the church needs to start a building fund," I said. "You'll need to get some land and start on a building if you expect any kind of growth at all."

"Now I might be able to peddle some church bonds," Jimmy Joe said. "What's the commission on those things?"

The man who called himself Jesus sighed. "It's not necessary that the CHURCH AMONG THE HUBCAPS, as you so aptly put it, survive as a building of brick and mortar. As I've told you before, the church is not cosmetic appearance."

"I know you mean well," I said, "but I don't think you have much understanding of the contemporary church. If your church is going to grow, you're going to have to promote, and you're going to have to find a better location. There are some people in this room who are willing to help you get this thing organized right."

Mary Lou chuckled, then sarcastically said, "As soon as you get Jesus and his church organized, you might want to think about getting your own life organized."

Sue Beth's unappreciated comment was, "Nice shot, Mary Lou."

"I hadn't really thought about church polo

leagues," Bum contributed, "but they're definitely a possibility. If I can help in that regard, Padre, don't hesitate to call on me."

"Thanks," the man who called himself Jesus half-heartedly replied.

"Church polo leagues are a dumb idea," Bobo said.

"Oh, I don't know about that," Chigger responded. "I don't see how anyone could object to playing polo for Jesus."

Sue Beth was supportive. "Chigger's right, and church polo leagues would offset some of the bad religious press horses have been getting for years."

"I didn't know horses had been getting bad press," Beep said. "I know mules have been getting bad press, but this is the first I've heard about horses."

The man who called himself Jesus left the room, I supposed to get dressed for the touch football game that was fast approaching. I admit to being a little nervous about the game. After all, our opponents would challenge us to the utmost of our abilities. We would all have to give one hundred percent to win the game.

"Well, what do you think of the guy?" I asked the group, referring to the man who called himself Jesus.

"He's nice, genuine," said Mary Lou. "If he wants to call himself Jesus, I don't see why you should object. In fact, I think he probably is Jesus."

I exclaimed, perhaps a little too loudly, "You've got to be kidding."

Sue Beth challenged, "I think everyone here thinks he's the real Jesus, except you."

"Now's the time for one or more of you clowns to confess," I said. "The joke has gone far enough."

Everyone gave me a blank stare, which isn't unusual for my friends. However, their failure to respond properly caused me to realize that one or more of them, perhaps all, wanted to keep the joke going. Well, if that was the way they wanted to play the game, it was fine with me.

Bobby Jack Lewis finally arrived, with the explanation that he'd had to tear himself away from several women. If not original, Bobby Jack is at least predictable.

"Are you ready to meet the Jesus imposter?" I asked.

Bobby Jack patted a brown paper sack he was carrying and replied, "I'm ready. With what I've got in this sack, I can determine if the guy is the real Jesus."

"I can tell you now that he isn't," I said, "but maybe your test will bring the clowns responsible for him out in the open."

I took Bobby Jack to the guest bedroom door, which was closed, and knocked. A voice from inside the room said, "Come in."

On entering the room, I apologized for disturbing him and said, "I just wanted you to meet Bobby

Jack Lewis."

He shook Bobby Jack's extended hand, and I swear there was a twinkle in his eyes when he asked, "Did you bring your lunch?" He was, of course, referring to the brown paper bag Bobby Jack was carrying.

Bobby Jack chuckled nervously, then said, "No, I just wanted to show you something."

From the sack, Bobby Jack took a small piece of cloth and a splinter of wood. Then he asked the man who called himself Jesus, "Do you recognize these items?"

"Am I supposed to?" the man asked.

"Yes, I would think so," Bobby Jack replied.

"I'm sorry to disappoint you, but to me it looks like you have an ordinary splinter of wood and an ordinary piece of cloth," the man said. He seemed amused by it all, like he knew what was coming next.

Bobby Jack shocked me when he said, "This splinter of wood is from the cross on which Jesus was crucified, and this piece of cloth is from the grave clothes he was wearing before he rose from the dead."

Flabbergasted, I asked, "Where did you get those things?"

"They were sent to me by a radio evangelist," he revealed.

For those unfamiliar with strong religious radio, there is a big clear channel station just across the

Rio Grande River from Del Rio, Texas. I used to catch religious broadcasts on it regularly, but have kind of gotten away from listening in recent years. For all I know, the station may no longer be operational.

The man who called himself Jesus laughed.

"What's so funny?" I asked. "It looks to me like Bobby Jack has nailed you."

"A poor choice of words," the man replied, "but until I saw this splinter, I didn't know the cross was made of mesquite. But then, I also didn't know the death shroud was polyester."

Bobby Jack had been duped by the radio evangelist, which had been brought to his attention in a less than subtle manner. He was embarrassed by the incident, and I felt sorry for him. Of course, I had known all along that what he presented was not a splinter from the cross or a piece of cloth from the death shroud. I'm not a gullible person.

I'll give Bobby Jack this. He had fired his best shot and it had been a dud, but he didn't fold. "What's your sign?" he asked the man who called himself Jesus.

"If you're talking about an astrological sign," the man said, "what difference does it make?"

Bobby Jack contended, "It makes a lot of difference. It's how I match people up in my dating service."

"What ever happened to marriages made in Heaven?" the man asked.

"You don't have to get married to get a date," I said.

"Anyway, what's your sign?" Bobby Jack reiterated.

"I don't see what difference it makes," the man said, "but from an earthly standpoint I would be a Gemini."

Bobby Jack exclaimed, "Aha! The real Jesus was born December Twenty-fifth, which would make him a Capricorn."

The man shook his head in resignation. "Have you ever been in Bethlehem in December?"

"I can't say as I have," Bobby Jack admitted.

"Well, if you had been there, you would know the shepherds wouldn't be out tending their flocks by night."

"Are you saying the Bible lied about Jesus being born December Twenty-fifth?" I challenged.

"There's nothing about December Twenty-fifth in the Bible," the man said.

"I was just testing you," I lied.

"I'm sure you were. Would you mind giving Bobby Jack and me some privacy. I'd like to talk to him . . . alone."

"No problem," I said, though I was a bit put out by the request. The guy was, after all, a guest in my house. "Remember that we play ball at one. You guys need to get ready."

"We'll be ready," he promised.

When I came out of the room, Mary Lou intercepted me and said, "Well?"

"Well what?"

"Did Bobby Jack prove he's not the real Jesus?"

"I've already proved that."

"How?"

"In lots of ways."

"How about naming one?"

"C'mon, Mary Lou. I don't have time to jack with you. I've got to put the barbecue sauce on the ribs."

She kept bugging me with questions, with incessant chatter. I just ignored her and took care of the more important work in the kitchen. Blackie, who was not with the other dogs, came in the kitchen and sniffed Mary Lou and me. I became a little jealous because he seemed to prefer her. I gave him some Cloret-flavored dog biscuits, which did little to help his fetid breath.

After a few minutes, Bobby Jack joined us in the kitchen.

"Well?" I asked.

"He's the real Jesus," Bobby Jack said.

XII

There is something about brown grass, grass burrs, a crisp winter day, and those moments just before a big game that brings out the best in me. Those moments before kickoff are a time of reflection, of sorrow for not having better prepared for a moment in history that can never be recaptured, and of determination to give one hundred and ten percent effort.

The butterflies, of course, flutter aimlessly in the ol' stomach, and I silently pray that the kickoff will come to me. After being touched, I know the butterflies will go away.

Prior to previous games, it had been my responsibility to give the pre-game pep talk, a responsibility that weighed heavily on me. After all, it is the pre-game talk that puts the team's mood in motion. And how the team responds in the first few minutes of conflict often sets the mood for the entire game.

For this upcoming and all-important game, I had asked Beep Jenkins to give the pre-game talk. Since Beep is from Oklahoma, I knew he had a solid grasp of the game and of what should be said to the team. I was not disappointed.

The field where we play is the undeveloped portion of a neighborhood park. It is uneven and has a definite slant to it. You're always running uphill or downhill, and the terrain accommodates numerous patches of grass burrs. If a man doesn't get burrs in his socks, you know he's not hustling.

Our team gathered at the upper end of the field for Beep's pre-game talk. Each of us found a place to sit devoid of stickers. Bobo sat on the big Igloo cooler, which was full of beer. He had a can in each hand.

Beep put a fresh chew of Beechnut in his mouth, spit a brown stream of tobacco juice and said, "Men, you know why you're here. Down at the other end of this field is a team that wants to beat the snot out of you. They're a team that knows nothing about the sacredness of a good coon hunt, a team that doesn't have America's best interest at heart. Hell, it wouldn't surprise me if they were all Communists."

We all glared downfield at our opponents, and some of them waved at us. It was as if they were mocking everything for which our team stood, which is truth, justice and the American way.

"Boys," Beep continued, "a good coon dog never gives up, no matter what the odds are against him. The good coon dog has set an example for you, so follow it. If people were more like coon dogs, the world would be a better place to live in.

"If there's ever going to be any peace in the world, if there's ever going to be any understanding, it's going to come about when people start following the example of a good coon dog."

I don't know how the rest of the guys felt, but Beep's words put a lump in my throat and tears in my eyes. Beep's emotion-charged words were enough to make a grown man cry.

He went on, "Most of you boys haven't been around the horn like me, but you're all good lads with lots of heart. And you gotta have heart, the heart of a good coon dog. It is that kind of heart that will bring you victory today.

"Look on your opponents today as mean, vicious coons that have to be brought to bay. Run your hearts out, block and touch as you know how, and victory will be yours."

By now Ribs was sobbing openly and Chigger was choking back the tears. Never had any of us been so touched.

The old coon hunter straightened his bent frame, spit another stream of tobacco, and said, "The entire free world is watching what is happening here today. It's not just a quest for victory, but your duty to play your hearts out."

It was then that I noticed the man who called himself Jesus, then that I saw he was smiling. He acted as though he was holding back a real guffaw. Seeing that he wasn't touched by Beep's words made me angry. The man had no shame in him, no heart.

"I've never asked for much out of life," Beep said. "Oh sure, I've made a few million and now have the best coon dog in the country, but these are things that God in His infinite wisdom gave me. He also cursed me with six wives who stole me blind and made life hell for my coon dogs. But it's not like me to blame God for my troubles. I don't have a bunch of boils festering up on me like . . . oh, never mind.

"I've only known you boys for a short time, but you're like family to me, as precious as my coon dogs. That's why I'm asking you to go out there today and win one for the Old Cooner. But no matter what happens, I'm proud of each and every one of you boys. If any of my wives had seen fit to give me sons, I would have wanted them to be just like you boys. With a couple of exceptions, of course. No offense to you, Ribs, or to you, Chico, but if I'd had boys colored up like you two, I'd have killed whichever of my wives produced them."

Both Ribs and Chico nodded agreement. They knew in their hearts that Beep was not making a racist statement. He was merely making a point, that being that he couldn't have been responsible for any off-color kids.

"It's time, boys," Beep said, "go out there and put them up a tree."

I went to the center of the field for the coin toss and stared at twelve-year-old Scoot Bailey. He is as mean a kid as you will ever want to meet.

"Hi, Mister Luther," he said. "Nice day, huh?"

I knew his greeting was meant to take me off guard, but I wasn't about to be deceived by the likes of him, especially after being so pumped up by

Beep's pre-game talk. "Forget the weather report, Scoot. Let's play ball."

"I could only get five other guys and my sister to play," he said.

"Tough teddy, Scoot. We've got eleven guys and we're coming at you with all eleven."

Scoot showed some surprise at the strong line I had taken. "Why don't you let us have a couple of your guys? That way it would be nine against nine."

"Forget it, Scoot. You knew this one was for all the marbles. You should have gotten your people together so you could field a full team."

Scoot shrugged his shoulders and came on with one of the oldest of all lines. "I thought we were going to choose up sides and play."

Those who don't know Scoot and his twin brother Skate could easily be mislead by their calm and seemingly good manners. But Bill Bailey's sons are very dangerous and intimidating touch football players. They ask no quarter, give none. There's a lot of speed, anger and muscle packed in their four-foot eleven-inch, almost hundred pound, bodies. Anytime they get a chance, they put a hard touch on you.

Snuff McGrew, who lives across from the field and usually officiates our Sunday touch football games, came ambling out to join Scoot and me. "How you boys doing?" he wanted to know.

Snuff is a squatty man who always has a pinch between his cheek and gum and a can of beer in one hand. He's a former NFL official who quit the game rather than have his judgment questioned by television instant replay. Snuff is a man of great principle whose decisions are law on the touch football field. He knows the game, loves it.

There are those who ignorantly claim that Snuff always leans our way on close decisions because the beer is on our side of the field. There is no truth to such tasteless remarks. Snuff is of all men most honorable. When he was officiating NFL games, he never steered me wrong once on the game he was officiating. He even let me lay a few bets for him.

"The weather being what it is, I don't see much point in a coin toss," Snuff said. "What do you want to do, Mark, kickoff or receive?"

"We'll receive," I said.

"Which end of the field do you want to defend?" Snuff asked.

Scoot said, "We'll take . . ."

"Shut up, Scoot," Snuff said. "Mark has the option here. Your lack of respect for your elders is going to cost you a penalty right off the bat. You have to kickoff from your goal line."

I was glad to see that Snuff was taking no guff, that he was taking control of the game from the outset. "We'll defend the goal up on the hill there," I said. It was a shrewd decision on my part, since my team would be running downhill on both offense and defense. The game would be an uphill battle for Scoot's team.

"Let's play ball," Snuff commanded.

Except for the man who called himself Jesus, my teammates showed great exuberance for the way I had handled the coin toss. I thought we had fared fairly well.

Beep got us all together and we all stacked hands on top of a fist he had made. We all expected him to say something profound and he didn't let us down. "Get 'em," he said. The way he said it sent chills running up and down my spine.

We took our positions on the field, except for Ribs, who stood on the sidelines and with his accordion played a polka rendition of *That Good Old Baylor Line*. It was a moment of rare ecstasy, and I couldn't understand why our cheerleaders, Mary Lou, Sue Beth, and Bumps were plopped down in lawn chairs chattering, eating and drinking. I have always suspected that cheerleaders know nothing about the game.

Snuff, who had sat down on our Igloo cooler after getting a can of beer out of it, gave the signal for the kickoff and Scoot put his foot into the pigskin. The ball took flight toward Bobo and I raced downfield looking for someone to block. The Ludlow boys, eleven-year-old Trike and ten-year-old Bike, were racing uphill toward Bobo. The Dunkin boys (no relation to the donut Dunkins), ten-year-old Porky and eleven-year-old Frog, were, along with Scoot and Skate, bearing down on Bobo. But it was the leader of the pack, the most dangerous toucher of them all, that I chose to block.

I tried to put a rolling body block into nine-year-old Sue Boo Bailey, but she deftly juked me and I rolled through a patch of grass burrs. Then I stared back uphill in horror as Bobo tried to make a one-handed catch of the kickoff, primarily because he had a can of beer in the other hand. The ball bounced off Bobo's head and tumbled toward the on-coming defenders. Skate pounced on it, drawing a whistle from Snuff, who got up from his seat on the Igloo and wandered back onto the field.

Careful not to spill his beer, Snuff hugged his chest with his arms and declared, "Illegal fumble recovery."

"Sir, I don't understand," Skate said.

"That will be a five-yard penalty," Snuff said, taking the ball and five giant steps downhill. Snuff knows how to quell a riot before it starts.

Offensively, I had the man who called himself Jesus and Ribs at the end positions, Jimmy Joe and Chico at tackles, Bobby Jack and Bum at guards, Bobo at center, Billy Bob and Joe Don as halfbacks, and Chigger at fullback.

In the huddle I told Ribs to run a fly pattern and the man who called himself Jesus to run a crossing pattern. "The rest of you block," I commanded. Looking downfield, I saw the *JOHN 3:16* sign at the back of the end zone.

As previously stated, we actually run a spread or short punt formation. From my position in the backfield, I looked across the line of scrimmage to try and determine what type of defense Scoot's troops were in, thinking I might have to change the play. But as is often the case, I had trouble recognizing Scoot's defense. He's a master of disguise.

Bobo's center snap took a nice bounce back to me, but out of the corner of eye I saw my worst fears coming to fruition. Sue Boo was blitzing and Bobo missed his block on her. I had to release my pass sooner than intended, and in the general direction of where I thought the man who called himself Jesus would be running.

The pass was behind the man, but he jumped, twisted, and made an unbelievable behind the head catch of the ball. Then, with moves that would have been the envy of Walter Payton, he juked both Porky and Frog and raced into the end zone.

For our extra point attempt, we let Chigger run a sweep to the right with everyone else blocking. But Sue Boo catapulted Jimmy Joe and gave Chigger a two-handed slap touch alongside the head.

At four-feet six-inches and upwards of fifty pounds, Sue Boo Bailey is not your average nine-year-old. The ponytail, freckles and sweet face may fool some people, but not me. The girl has a mean streak in her, and more than once Snuff has had to throw her out of a game for being too aggressive.

Snuff had been busy getting a beer and talking to Mary Lou and Sue Beth when we scored and tried for the extra point, so he was surprised to see us lining up to kickoff to Scoot's team. "What's going on?" he wanted to know.

"We scored," I explained.

"Seven to zip, huh?"

"No, we missed the extra point."

He grumbled, "Damn. Next time tell me when you're trying for the point after and you might make it."

Though the rest of the team had high-fived the man who called himself Jesus following his touchdown, I had been too busy planning the extra point attempt. Now I thought it important to give him a pat on the back and tell him he had made a good catch and run.

"Thanks," he said. "Next time lead me a little and I won't have to make like a pretzel to catch the ball."

I had figured him to be a little more grateful for the pass I delivered with the type pressure being put on me by Sue Boo. It just goes to show that quarterback is the most misunderstood position in touch football.

Bum's our kickoff man, and he really pounded the football. It went rotating end-over-end down the hill and to the goal line of our opponents, where it was fielded by Trike Ludlow. The speedy Trike pedaled straight up the center of the field until our entire team converged on him, then he streaked toward the sideline and back up the field. With a rolling block Skate had wiped out Ribs and Chico, and Sue Boo leveled Jimmy Joe, Billy Bob, Joe Don and Bobby Jack. The rest of us had been left in Trike's wake, so I feared he would score. But Trike hadn't counted on Bobo's guile. Our big center had gone over to the Igloo to get himself a beer, so as Trike sped up the sideline he ran right into Bobo as he was coming back onto the field.

"Nice play," I yelled at Bobo.

"Huh?" he replied. Bobo's not one to revel in his guile.

Frankly, I thought Sue Boo's block, which took out four of my guys, was illegal. However, I didn't call it to Snuff's attention because he was entertaining Mary Lou and Sue Beth, balancing a can of beer on his nose. Snuff gets irritable when someone interrupts one of his tricks.

Snuff was still busy with his trick when Scoot, Skate, Bike and Trike pulled an illegal triple reverse that ended with a pass to Sue Boo for a touchdown. With exception of the man who called himself Jesus, our guys were all winded by the time the play ended. That's why Frog Dunkin was able to hop into the end zone for the extra point, giving Scoot's team a one point lead.

I suspicioned that the man who called himself Jesus could have stopped the pass play and the extra point. But I'm not one to judge, especially on Sunday.

As we lined up to receive the kickoff, I glanced over and saw Beep prowling the sideline, pacing like an indecisive coon. I could see the worry etched on his brow. But he clapped his hands and shouted words of encouragement to us. I'm sure it bothered Beep that Mary Lou and Sue Beth hadn't bothered to give one fight yell. Sue Beth was too busy working on a drumstick, and Mary Lou was polishing her nails. And Snuff was taking a nap, a can of beer balanced on his forehead.

Scoot's uphill kick was one of those low bouncing jobs that is difficult to handle. Chico scooped it and started racing downfield. He was in the process of picking up big yardage when all of a sudden he stopped in his tracks, dropped the football and ran out of bounds. Porky Dunkin made the recovery for Scoot's team.

Chico's attention had been diverted from football to a shiny hubcap lying in the grass just off the field. He had picked it up and was examining it while I was screaming at him. He didn't pay any attention to me, though, just trotted over to his car and put the hubcap in the trunk.

Sue Boo's devious smile did not go unnoticed. I suspected she was responsible for the hubcap lying in the grass.

Scoot's team started pounding away at us, but we defended the hill with honor. It took another triple reverse by Scoot, Skate, Bike and Trike, who pitched back to Porky, who passed to Frog, who lateraled to Sue Boo, before they were able to score. It was a play we knew they had in their bag of tricks, and we thought we knew how to defend it, but they executed to perfection.

I was proud of the way the team was performing, though I don't think the man who called himself Jesus was putting as much into the game as the rest of us. He had, of course, caused considerable suspicion with statements about God not caring who wins football games. I believe that God does care. I knew in my heart that God wouldn't allow a group of juvenile delinquents to beat us.

With an all-out blitz, we were able to stop Scoot's team from making the extra point, but we were still trailing thirteen to six and half-time was fast approaching.

Scoot's kickoff came skittering up the hill and was fielded by Chigger, who started racing downfield and just flat disappeared from my sight. Scoot, Skate, Bike, Trike, Porky, Frog and Sue Boo must have lost sight of him, too, because they started wandering aimlessly, like they were in search of Easter eggs.

Suddenly, Chigger darted from behind Bobo, where he had been hiding, and raced for the end zone. He had just one man to beat, that being Sue Boo Bailey, who was in hot pursuit. Billy Bob Raintree, all his legal training coming to bear, tried to clip Sue Boo from behind, but instead burrowed his head into the ground and a patch of grass burrs.

Chigger darted and dodged, but could not shake the tenacious Sue Boo. Granted, Chigger looks like he's running faster than he is, which is the case with all short people. But I'll give Chigger this, he was giving his all. But then Sue Boo was in front of him, slapping him upside the head.

The girl is the Dick Butkus of touch football. After Chigger fell to the turf from exhaustion and her head slap, she just stood there glowering at him. Never mind that she said, "Are you okay, Mister Dodgen?" She didn't really have a gnat's concern for Chigger.

Though Chigger didn't score, he gave us good field position. I figured it was time for our first gimmick play of the day. I'm like coaches Tom Landry of the Dallas Cowboys and Don Shula of the Miami Dolphins on that score. I always have a special play for that critical moment in a game. So, I called quadruple reverse, shovel pass, triple lateral.

The play is not as complicated as it sounds. Bobo snaps the ball to me, I run to the right and hand off to Ribs, who runs to the left and hands off to Billy Bob, who runs to the right and hands off to Joe Don, who runs to the left and hands off to the man who called himself Jesus, who runs to the right and shovel passes to Jimmy Joe, who laterals to Bobby Jack, who laterals to Bum, who laterals to Chico. We run several variations of the play.

Anyway, I called the play, took a two-hop snap from Bobo, and Sue Boo broke through the line and slapped me upside the head before I could even get started running to the right.

I glared at the man who called himself Jesus when he said, "I didn't think that play would work."

I challenged him with "Do you want to start calling the plays?"

"Sure," he replied. "throw me the ball on a crossing pattern and we can go in tied at half-time."

"You've got it," I said, angrily.

Bobo's snap sailed over my head, but I ran back and took it on the first bounce, then launched a blind throw downfield. The man who called himself Jesus caught the ball behind his back with one hand and waltzed into the end zone.

Our guys were so excited that they all ran down into the end zone, high-fived him, jumped on him and made him the bottom of the pile. I didn't join them, primarily because I was still a little ticked about him challenging my authority. And we still had an extra point to make to tie the score. Someone had to keep a cool head, and that someone had to be me.

The man who called himself Jesus came out of the pile grinning, which also didn't set too well with me. It was like he was gloating, which is something I can't abide in a grown man.

For the extra point, I called a fake reverse and carried the ball into the end zone myself. This enabled me to stick my tongue out at Sue Boo Bailey and spike the ball at her feet. I could tell she was deflated when she said. "Is it half-time yet, Mister Luther? I have to go to the bathroom."

It was, indeed, half-time. We had scored on the last play of the half, which usually spells the death knell for the opposing team. They lose heart, can't seem to get it going in the second half.

Beep gathered us on the sideline where Mary Lou and Sue Beth were seated. We toweled ourselves, drank Gatorade, and listened attentively as Beep analyzed some of the problems we had experienced in the first half. We had trouble hearing Beep because of Snuff's snoring, so we had to move.

"As a head coach, I've got one main objective," Beep said. "It's up to me to dig, claw, wheedle and coax a fanatical effort out of you boys. I want you boys to play like you're planting the flag on Iwo Jima."

A low rumble of appreciation filtered through the team, which I interpreted as a commitment to excellence. Whether for one minute or more, I believe Beep is the best manager I've ever met.

However, I don't think any of that rumble of appreciation came from the man who called himself Jesus. He always seemed to find Beep's talks amusing, not inspirational. I got the distinct impression that he was the kind of guy who would go off half-cocked, would be easily led by false prophets. That's why I found it impossible to believe he was who he claimed to be.

Knowing how much victory meant to us, Beep had gone over to my house, which was nearby, and gotten Oklahoma Crude out of my backyard. He let each of us rub the dog's head for luck. Ribs offered to let us rub his head, too, but everyone declined. We chose, instead, to rub Blackie's head. Blackie had been witness to the entire first half, lying at Sue Beth's feet and eating her leftovers. He was so full he couldn't move.

Just before time for the second half kickoff, Beep again got us to stack our hands on his fist, and he prayed this prayer, "Lord, there are times when we haven't done exactly as you'd want us to do, but these boys here are playing their hearts out for you. They want to win this game for Your Glory, Lord, not their own. That's why I don't feel bad about asking for your help. Help them to defeat the Red Menace, which, I have on good authority, are supporting their opponents. You wouldn't want Communism to get a foothold on this field now, would You, Lord? No, we know You wouldn't. We know You hate Communism the way a good coon dog hates an old rogue coon. So give us the victory, Lord, and we'll give You the glory. Now and forever, amen."

Some of us, touched by Beep's words, were weeping openly. But I swear the man who called himself Jesus was chuckling.

Before we unstacked our hands, Beep gave us his scintillating "Get 'em" We broke onto the field, each and every man with a deep commitment to win the game for the *Big Coon Hunter in the Sky.*

Snuff had awakened for the second half and another beer. He again gave me the choice on kicking or receiving and the choice of goal lines to defend. I pondered by options carefully, then chose to receive and defend the goal line at the top of the hill. When Scoot objected, Snuff penalized him back to his own goal line at the bottom of the hill.

Scoot kicked the ball long and deep. It settled in Bum Criswell's arms and he started forward carefully, his riding boots pounding the sod in the chill of the afternoon. Here he was, one horseman minus a horse, but with the determination of the *Four Horsemen of the Apocalypse.*

We all crowded around Bum, forming an impenetrable flying wedge, which I thought would knife through our opponents and carry Bum across the goal line. But Sue Boo Bailey went around the wedge, got inside it with Bum, and slapped him upside the head.

Her entrance into the wedge was obviously illegal, but when I looked to Snuff for help, he was again asleep, a can of beer balanced on his stomach. The kid's disregard for accepted rules of touch football was making me angry, but I was determined not to let her rattle me.

Mary Lou, Sue Beth and Bumps had finally gotten out of their lawn chairs, I thought to give us a cheer. But they were only stretching. They were soon back in their chairs, oblivious to the importance of what was happening on the field of play.

Beep, on the other hand, God bless him, was pacing, clapping his hands and yelling words of encouragement. Oklahoma Crude had joined Blackie at Sue Beth's feet.

In the huddle I said, "Okay, guys, quadruple reverse, shovel pass, triple lateral."

The man who called himself Jesus chuckled, but I didn't pay any attention to him. The quadruple reverse, shovel pass, triple lateral is a good play. It hadn't worked the first time it was called because Sue Boo Bailey hadn't been blocked. But Bobo had made a commitment to *cream her* if I called the play again. When Bobo's riled, he's as tough a touch football player as ever laced on a pair of Nikes.

Maybe it was Bobo's obsession with *creaming* Sue Boo, or maybe a perspiring beer can had made his hand wet and slippery. Whatever the reason, Bobo again centered the ball over my head.

He also missed his block on Sue Boo Bailey and *creamed* Bobby Jack Lewis. Sue Boo bolted right past me, caught the long center snap while it was still in the air, and trotted into the end zone. The advantage we had enjoyed by scoring just before the first half ended was gone. Momentum had swung back to Scoot's team.

Fortunately, we were able to foil the extra point attempt. Scoot tried to hit Frog with a pass in the flat, but Joe Don stuck out a foot and tripped the receiver. Scoot protested, of course, but by a vote of ten to eight we overrode his contention that it was pass interference. The man who called himself Jesus voted with Scoot's team.

With the score now nineteen to thirteen, I knew we faced a downhill battle to tie or gain the lead.

On the ensuing kickoff, Scoot boomed the ball deep up the hill where it was fielded by Joe Don. He lateraled to Chigger and, with Bobo, tried to level the onrushing Sue Boo Bailey. Their plan was to catch her in a vise block, but she zipped between them and they crashed into each other. Whether they were knocked senseless or not was difficult to determine, given their normal mental state. Regardless, Sue Boo slapped Chigger upside the head before he 'could really get started.

In the huddle, I was about to call the play when Bobby Jack said, "Why don't you let Jesus call the play?"

There was a chorus of "amens" from the other players, which angered me a great deal. Even if the guy was the real Jesus, which he wasn't, I considered myself better equipped to call the plays. I didn't mind praying to God for victory, but I didn't want Him calling the plays, either.

The clincher came, though, when from the sideline Beep hollered out, "Let Jesus call the play."

"Yeah, let Jesus call the play," chorused Mary Lou, Sue Beth and Bumps. Then the trio started chanting, "We want Jesus. We want Jesus."

For me, it was humiliating; almost like a loss. Here was a man who had been a head coach for a day, wanting me to give up my play calling, something I had done for years. He was ready on a whim to make the man who called himself Jesus the offensive coordinator.

And Mary Lou, Sue Beth, and Bumps, who hadn't bothered to provide any *fight* yells all day, suddenly calling for the man who called himself Jesus to take control of the team.

With my most obvious sulking voice I said, "I don't care who calls the plays. I just want to win the game."

I am first and foremost a team player.

The man who called himself Jesus called a play I was sure wouldn't work. I was to throw a buttonhook pass to Ribs, who would lateral to the man who called himself Jesus.

The play was perfection. I threw a tight spiral to Ribs, who flipped back to the man who called himself Jesus, who rambled untouched into the end zone. I got so caught up in the emotion of my teammates, the fact we had tied the score, that I forgot my previous anger. The way the man could run, the way he could catch the ball, the fact that he played what might be considered mistake-free touch football, caused me to momentarily believe that he might really be Jesus Christ.

The extra point seemed almost an afterthought, a guard around pass from Bobby Jack to Billy Bob. We suddenly had a one point lead, twenty to nineteen.

But Scoot's team was not ready to give up. After we kicked off and touched Frog Dunkin down about mid-field, Scoot initiated a relentless ground attack with the fleet Sue Boo Bailey carrying the ball behind some devastating blocking. I didn't think anyone could run through our defensive line, and I was right on that score. The cunning Sue Boo, playing her usual dirty brand of touch football, kept running around our line.

In short order, Scoot's troops marched up the hill, with Sue Boo scoring on an end sweep. She defiantly spiked the ball at my feet.

I got in the last taunt, though, when Bobo broke past Trike Ludlow's block and nailed Sue Boo in the backfield, keeping our adversaries from making the extra point. Scoot claimed Bobo was off sides, that he had gotten into their backfield before the ball was centered. We overruled Scoot's objection by a vote of ten to eight. The man who called himself Jesus voted with Scoot's team, which didn't win him any friends.

We were down twenty-five to twenty, but with time for one more drive. With the man who called himself Jesus on our side, I was confident that we could march down the hill and score.

Scoot's kick was a dribbler that came right up the middle of the field. Bobo tried to field it, couldn't, so he fell on the ball. All the air went out of it.

Fortunately, Scoot had brought his ball. It was new, suspicious, didn't have the character of the ball we had been using. Before putting it into play, Beep insisted on inspecting it, just to make sure it was American-made.

"You never know what a Commie might try to pull," Beep explained. "To hear them tell it, they invented coon hunting."

I didn't like the feel of the new ball, but sometimes a man has to deal with adversity. From my perspective, having to use a strange ball was just another obstacle to overcome, another victory to be won. I adhere to the old adage, "When the going gets tough, the tough get going."

My teammates didn't object when I called the play. They were, perhaps, upset with the man who called himself Jesus for siding with Scoot's team on the alleged penalty against Bobo.

Three times I called ingenious plays, only to see them thwarted by the rock-ribbed defense of our opponents. Sue Boo Bailey was playing middle linebacker with a fanatical zeal that bordered on frenzy.

Then there was time for only one more play. The game, possibly the continued freedom of the entire nation rested on the outcome of that one play. With everything on the line, I decided it was time to start believing in the man who called himself Jesus.

"Okay, Jesus," I said, "run a fly pattern and I'll hit you in the end zone." He gave me a funny look, because up until this critical time I had never accepted him as the real Jesus, never called him by that name.

The play worked beautifully. Jimmy Joe, Billy

Bob, Bobo and Joe Don blocked out the blitzing Sue Boo, and I arched a beautiful spiral that landed right in the hands of the man who called himself Jesus.

And he dropped it.

I screamed. I fell down on the ground and rolled around in frustration while Scoot, Sue Boo and the rest of our opponents celebrated. I was of all men most miserable.

I might possibly have rolled around in the grass burrs for days, but I finally looked up and the man who called himself Jesus was offering me a hand. He also provided some cheerless words.

"I'm sorry, Mark, but I can't be who you want me to be. God can't be who you want Him to be."

XIII

Because of the loss, the spareribs had lost their savor; though in truth, no one seemed to notice except me. My guests all wolfed down the food with relish, whereas I had a lump in my chest and tears in my eyes that prohibited me from enjoying the meal. Losing is difficult for me, and especially losing to an arch rival like Scoot.

To the others, I guess it was just another game. It was obviously just another game to the man who called himself Jesus. He seemed very content and laid-back, serving food to all the guests and making sure they had everything they wanted. As for my attitude toward him, I was still miffed about the way he had muffed the pass, and with his cavalier, "I can't be who you want me to be. God can't be who you want him to be."

Hell, all I expected him to be was a decent pass receiver. I sure didn't expect him to be who he claimed to be, not the Son of God. And as for God not being who I want him to be, I sure don't understand that statement.

I know this. If we had won, I would have been more than willing to have given God some of the credit. After all, I believe in praying before a game and asking for God's help. It was the man who called himself Jesus, not me, who had said God isn't interested in football. I've always thought of football as a priority item with God, though I would be the first to admit that God probably isn't as interested in the point spread as I am. However, I happen to know that some of the gamblers who establish the point spread on games pray long and hard before coming to a decision. I don't find that unusual, since a lot of people pray for success in their professions.

One thing I couldn't understand were all my friends complimenting the man who called himself Jesus for the game he had played. Sure, he had scored three touchdowns, but he had choked in the clutch. My ol' high school coach taught me that no matter how well you play in a game, a mistake negates all the good you did. He was a man who really understood football, the serious implications of the game. He likened the game to life, always taught us the game builds character.

One of the greatest character-building lessons he ever taught us was in preparation for a championship game. The other team had a great running back, and he assigned some of us to take him out anyway we could. We were fortunate enough to break the guy's leg on the opening kickoff.

Anyway, regarding the man who called himself Jesus, if he had made the crucial catch, I might have been almost ready to believe he was the real Jesus. However, his failure to come through when the game was on the line reinforced my belief that he was a charlatan. The real Jesus would have caught the ball. He wouldn't have allowed a bunch of Commie kids to beat us.

"Lighten up, Mark," Bobo said between guzzle-like swigs of beer. "We played a helluva good game. Nobody expected us to win, but we did beat the spread."

"Yeah," I conceded, "but we could have done more than beat the spread. We could have won the game if the man who claims to be Jesus had caught the ball."

"I can't find any fault with the man," Bobo said. "He made some supernatural catches."

"Maybe so," I agreed, "but he also made the biggest boo boo of the game, and that makes me know he's not who he claims to be. As for what you call supernatural catches, he was just lucky."

Bobo shook his head in disagreement. "You're wrong, Mark."

"Hey, the day you give up brew is the day I'll believe he's the real Jesus."

"You really know how to hurt a guy," Bobo said.

On that score Bobo is right. Verbally, I do know how to hurt someone, which I consider to be one of my strong suits. And while I had humored the man who called himself Jesus, gone along with the gag someone was playing, his screwing up our chance for victory had caused me to reevaluate. The situation was no longer funny, and I was more than a little teed off at whoever had sent him my way.

There are those who claim I became angry, sullen and abusive following the game. While it's true I was hitting the sauce pretty heavy, the one thing I can do is handle my liquor. For that reason, I don't give much substance to the aforementioned report regarding my after-game personality. Though I was, and continue to be, miffed at losing to Scoot's team, I was not, as Mary Lou said, acting like an asshole.

It's true that I asked Beep Jenkins to get his dogs out of my hot tub, but I hardly think of that as being abusive. I even made a joke out of it, told Beep that as long as the dogs were in the tub they might as well share a good bottle of wine, too.

Beep didn't even pay any attention to my request. He filled his plate with spareribs, went out on the deck, stripped down to his birthday suit, and joined the dogs in the hot tub. He stayed there until the entire Cowboys-Eagles game was over.

Though the others were too calloused to realize it, I think the loss to Scoot's team really took its toll on Beep. He was heartbroken about the defeat, told me he was giving up coaching touch football and would stick to coon hunting.

"If I ever coach again," Beep said, "it will be with the understanding that I call the plays. Where do you think we went wrong, Mark? What did we do that made God turn his back on us?"

I shrugged my shoulders. "Beats me. As far as

I'm concerned, the game was dedicated to His Glory."

It was then I started suspecting Beep might actually have been aspiring to a career as an NFL coach. The man had the charisma to be a great one.

Beep said he had hoped to find another outlet, in addition to coon hunting, to occupy some of his time, but that he guessed God didn't want him in coaching.

"There's not much point to daytime coon hunting," Beep informed. "Oh, you can do it, romanticize the dickens out of it, but you rarely find a coon. It's just not what it's cracked up to be."

I agreed with Beep that daytime coon hunting didn't stir and inspire me like nighttime coon hunting. Of course, I had only been that one time, and it was at night. Maybe it's all a matter of what you get use to.

Beep surprised me when he said, "I've given some serious thought to being a male stripper. Do you think I've got the body for it?"

I told Beep that while he did, indeed, have the body to be a male stripper, it was my understanding that most of them worked at night, which would hinder his coon hunting. Beep informed me that he had discovered a couple of daytime hangouts for housewives that employed male strippers.

"The money's not important," he said. "I just want to do something that's fulfilling, satisfying.

And, of course, the only way I'd take a job as a stripper is if they would allow my dogs to stay backstage."

I told Beep I didn't think anyone could possibly object to his dogs staying backstage, but wondered if it was the right kind of environment for them. In fact, I told him I wondered if my hot tub was the right kind of environment for them.

Beep certainly had no cause to think I was sullen, angry and abusive following our game. If anything, I was very supportive of Beep. I'm only sorry that I didn't have a solution to his dilemma regarding a secondary career.

Admittedly, I did get a little ill-tempered with Bum Criswell, but only after he showed no concern about his horse kicking down part of my fence. Bum said I was overly concerned about the fence, that it could be easily repaired. When I asked if he planned to pay for the repairs, he claimed a horse kicking down a fence was an *Act of God,* thereby negating his responsibility.

I told Bum that God didn't put the horse in my yard.

He whined, "I'd pay for the fence if I had the money, but you know all my funds are tied up in polo. And now I feel a deep commitment to start a Christian polo league. I plan to talk to Jesus about it."

I made a suggestion as to where Bum could stick his mallet, or whatever that thing is that they use in polo.

"You have a very un-Christian attitude," he told me. "I don't think I'll be inviting you to join the Fellowship of Christian Polo Players."

I told Bum there was already a Fellowship of Christian Athletes, which I hadn't been invited to join either, and that I saw little, if any, need for a Fellowship of Christian Polo Players. He said the athletic skill required in polo was so superior to that required in other sports that polo players would not be satisfied with anything less than their own Christian athletes group.

I suggested the possibility of polo players having a different kind of athletes foot and jock itch, too, and further said the horses were more athletic than the persons who rode them. This didn't set too well, but I think what really hurt Bum's feelings was my contention that the man who called himself Jesus would laugh at his idea of Christian polo leagues.

Whatever the reason, Bum got that stupid hurt look on his face, which prompted Mary Lou and Sue Beth to get on my case. Both made reference to me being a pompous ass. In looking back on all that happened, it was not my best day.

Then Bobby Jack Lewis, who had made the transition from doubter to a dyed-in-the-wool disciple of the man who called himself Jesus, started blaming me for the loss to Scoot's team. This was more than a little hard for me to take since, due to his religious upbringing and flirtation with the charismatic supernatural, I had counted on Bobby Jack's support.

"The man who calls himself Jesus had victory right in his hands and lost it," I complained.

Bobby Jack contended, "It should never have come down to the last play. If you had put together a decent game play, we would have won by three or four touchdowns."

I grumbled, "There was nothing wrong with the game plan. We hadn't planned on Sue Boo Bailey playing for Scoot's team. If you guys had knocked her out of the game, maybe broken her leg, the game plan would have worked to perfection."

But Chico Neiman Marcus agreed with Bobby Jack, that it was my game plan that was responsible for the loss, not the man who called himself Jesus. Of course, I expected something like that from Chico. He had become completely enamored with the man who called himself Jesus, this in spite of the fact that the man looked nothing like any of the pictures of the real Jesus in Chico's mother's Bible.

I have great respect for artists, whether they work on canvas or black velvet. And because artists, like writers, have inspiration from above, I figure their pictures of Jesus are pretty accurate, especially the King James Version pictures. I admit that I don't have much confidence in the pictures in the Communist-inspired versions of the Bible. There is only one true version, only one version that God authorized, and that's the King James.

That, of course, brings up another minus factor

for the man who called himself Jesus. He did not speak in King James Version English like the real Jesus did.

With Bobby Jack and Chico critical of my game plan, I turned to the only truly great football mind in the room other than my own.

"Okay, Ribs, what did you think of my game plan?"

"It sucked," he said. Blackie nodded his head in agreement.

Now it is one thing for Bobby Jack and Chico to be critical, but quite another for Ribs to find fault with me. After all, I taught the man everything he knows about touch football. I took a raw piece of talent and molded him into one of the finest touch football receivers in North Dallas. And a black man should never question the game plan of a white man. Such questioning could well be the reason the world is in the shape it is in today.

I argued, "You've got no call to be critical of my game plan. The game was lost because of poor execution, not my game plan."

"Think again," Joe Don said. "My mother could have drawn up a better game plan."

The guys had never been this mutinous before. I had to think the man who called himself Jesus was responsible for their attitude change. I was beginning to think he was not only a charlatan, but also a troublemaker. That was another strike against him, since I was pretty sure the real Jesus wouldn't cause any trouble.

Even Chigger got on my case, which is not like him. He is normally wise beyond his height. He learned at a very young age that the top of his head is at the perfect height to be hammered by a normal-size man. Not being one of violent persuasion, I had never given much thought to doing any hammering on Chigger's head, until he got on my case. Of course, any thought of violence to Chigger's person was tempered by the knowledge that Sue Beth was in the room. And she outweighs me by fifty or so pounds.

"Let's face it, Hoss," Jimmy Joe Johnson said, "it should never have come down to that last desperation pass. We should have been playing prevent defense by the third quarter."

Billy Bob Raintree said, "I'm going to have to agree with Jimmy Joe. I don't think there's a jury in the country that could be convinced that you had a good game plan."

It was then that the man who called himself Jesus came to my rescue with, "The important thing to remember, Mark, is that the game and the game plan were not important. There are many things that are more important."

Easy for him to say, I thought. The man was always speaking in riddles.

XIV

The man who called himself Jesus made grits for breakfast the next morning. I thought maybe he was feeling bad about dropping the pass, and about the way my friends had gotten on my case the day before. But over coffee and grits he told me he thought it best if he moved out of the house.

I shrugged my shoulders. "Well, if you don't feel comfortable here . . ."

He laughed. "I think it's more a matter of you feeling comfortable than me."

"Where will you go?"

"Chico's going to provide me a room down at the store."

"That's kind of a grubby place."

"It will be fine," he assured.

When I got home from work that night, he was gone. In fact, there was no evidence he had ever been in the place. He had thoroughly cleaned the house and the yard, and had repaired the fence kicked down by Bum's horse. He had even emptied, cleaned and refilled the hot tub.

Though he had only stayed at the house a week and a day, it seemed strange that he was no longer there. Of course, I didn't miss him or anything like that. Mostly, he had been a pain and an inconvenience, in spite of his domestic ability. As I've mentioned before, I like living alone.

After a couple of drinks, I decided to call Mary Lou. She answered after a couple of rings and I asked her if she would like to join me for dinner.

"Sorry," she said, "Sue Beth, Chigger and I are going down to Chico's to help Jesus get settled in."

"Why are you doing that?" I wanted to know.

"Well, you kicked him out of your house. It's the least we can do."

"I didn't kick him out of my house. He's lying if he said that."

"Oh, he didn't say you kicked him out. But that's the way I interpret what happened. You can make a person feel pretty unwelcome in your life."

Arguing with Mary Lou is futile. Her head is so hard it could be used for an anvil.

"Chico's place is in a kind of rough area," I said. "Maybe I ought to go with you."

"Never mind," she responded, coldly. "I'm sure Chigger will be more than adequate protection."

I laughed. "You've got to be kidding."

"No, I'm not kidding at all," she said. "Besides, with Jesus and Chico there, we'll be perfectly safe."

"I wish you'd quit calling that guy Jesus. He's just an actor. A good one, admittedly, but just an actor."

"You're sure of that, huh?"

I affirmed, "I'm sure. I'm just not sure why the

joker, or jokers, who hired the guy haven't admitted to it yet. The joke's over."

"The joke's always been over," Mary Lou responded.

What she meant by that, I don't know. I learned long ago not to even try to interpret Mary Lou Magruder. She is a complex woman, one whose weird mind defies amateur analysis.

Since Mary Lou was unavailable, I decided to give Bobo a call. He wouldn't be interested in chowing down, but I could entice him to join me for a few brews.

"Sorry," Bobo's wife told me over the telephone, "he went to someone named Chico's place. I think it's down on Harry Hines."

I wasn't believing what was happening here, but if nothing else I'm persistent. I called Ribs and got no answer, then Billy Bob's and Jimmy Joe's places and got the same results.

Then I remembered the one guy I could count on to put the feedbag on with me. I dialed Joe Don's number. He answered, but sounded out of breath. When I spelled out my plan, he informed me that he was on his way to Chico's, that he had been outside the door and rushed back in to take my call.

I told Joe Don that it seemed to me Chico had rounded up more than enough people to put a room in order for the man who called himself Jesus, that he would probably just be in the way.

"After tossing him out like you did, I feel obligated to help," he said.

I denied tossing the man out of my house, but Joe Don wasn't buying my denial. "I know how you are," he said. "You can make things pretty uncomfortable for a person, even a friend."

Exasperated, I replied, "I don't care what you believe, there's still no point in you going down to Chico's place. We can head over to Highland Park Cafeteria and chow down on the upstairs buffet. I'm buying."

"Thanks, but no thanks. I want to talk to Jesus while I've got the chance."

"What do you mean?"

"He's not going to hang around here forever, you know," Joe Don answered.

"As far as I'm concerned, he can't get out of town fast enough. And I can't believe you're buying that phony Jesus act. C'mon, Joe Don, tell me what's going on."

"If you weren't so blind and arrogant, you could see what's going on."

It was obvious I wasn't getting anywhere with Joe Don, so I told him to enjoy his trip to Harry Hines, and that it would be a cold day in hell before I invited him to dinner again. He just chuckled, told me he appreciated the invitation and hoped that I would eventually wake up. I told him I was awake, sober, and didn't need any mothering.

I next called Bum Criswell at home, but there was no answer. That prompted me to call him on his cellular saddle phone. That's right, some people have car phones and Bum has what might be called a horse or saddle phone. He answered almost immediately.

"Bum, old buddy, what are you up to?"

"Is that you, Mark?"

"Yeah, it's me."

"You'll have to speak up. I'm galloping down Beltline Road and the traffic is pretty noisy."

I increased my volume a few octaves and said, "If you're not busy, I'd like to take you to dinner tonight."

"Thanks, I appreciate it, but I just rode through a Burger King and picked up a couple of flame broiled burgers. My horse won't eat burgers that aren't flame broiled."

They say confession is good for the soul, so I confessed to Bum that I didn't know about his horse's affinity for flame broiled burgers. "A little ol' burger isn't going to tide you over, Bum. Let's go somewhere and really chow down."

"Can't tonight, I'm on my way to Chico's."

This left me with no one to call except Bobby Jack Lewis, the man who had betrayed me and strayed into the camp of the man who called himself Jesus. I called and his answering service told me he had gone to Chico's.

XV

For the next few days, I had trouble making contact with any of my alleged friends. I discovered that all of them were spending their spare time at the CHURCH AMONG THE HUBCAPS, and in the company of the man who called himself Jesus.

As a result of their new association, they were missing some of the best parties of the year, the chance to really celebrate Christ's birth. The Christmas season is appealing because everyone is generous and willing to share their best booze. Though I never get drunk, of course, I keep a nice buzz on from mid-December until the first couple of days in January. Sometime just prior to the first of the year, I make my New Year's resolutions, one of them being to cut down on the drinking and another to start seriously jogging. I've been making these resolutions for more years than I care to remember.

It certainly didn't bother me that my alleged friends had forsaken me for the man who called himself Jesus. Frankly, I had been wanting to spend Christmas alone for some time, and their rejection of me would also reduce my expenses. I had always given each of them a nice gift for Christmas, but now I didn't feel obligated to give any of them a damn thing.

I hadn't seen the man who called himself Jesus since that morning when he told me he was moving out, and I wasn't interested in seeing him ever again. He is not my kind of people. Still, I was curious enough about his activities to ask one of the paper's entertainment critics to visit the CHURCH AMONG THE HUBCAPS, and to give me a review of what was going on. I was quite pleased with his report.

"I have to agree with you that the man isn't the real Jesus," the critic told me.

"You don't have to convince me," I said, "but on what are you basing your evaluation?"

"Well, the place was packed," he replied, "and everyone seemed to be enjoying themselves."

"And that's why you say he isn't Jesus?"

He haughtily responded. "Hey, you asked me to go down there and use the criteria I use for reviewing a movie, book or play. One of my criteria is that if people enjoy it and understand it, it's no good. This guy who calls himself Jesus, he makes too much sense and is too easy to understand to be real. Also, he's not from New York, so we can assume he doesn't know what he's talking about."

"Of course," I said. "Why didn't I think of that? He would have to be from New York or somewhere up east to be credible."

"That's right," the critic said.

"Well, I really appreciate you going down there and checking things out for me, and I'm glad to know how you review things. I do have another un-related question."

"Shoot," he said.

"Not too long ago, I heard someone on television ask Stephen King when he was going to write a serious work. Would you mind telling me how you determine whether or not something is a serious work?"

"Not at all," the critic replied. "First of all the author would either have to live in New York or be dead. And even if he's dead, he would have to have spent time in New York. And it goes without saying that the book would have to be one no one wants to read. A serious book is assigned reading, usually by an English teacher."

"And a movie is judged the same way?" I asked.

"Basically," he said, "except that the better mov-ies have to be foreign. My job as a critic is to make everyone who doesn't watch public television and listen to classical music seem like an ignorant slob. That's pretty easy to do.

"For light reading, you should only read self-help books recommended by *The New York Times.*"

"This is helpful information," I said. "Now I'll know how to judge things for myself."

My critic friend's comments made me feel good because I am a foreign film buff. I try to catch every Japanese-made Godzilla film that comes out. His revelation also caused me to ponder my brief relationship with the man who called himself Jesus.

On that first night I had met him, he had hit me with some pretty heavy religious stuff. Of course, I had been equal to it. In any give-and-take situation, I've always been able to hold my own. But I still wondered about my willingness to listen to him on that night. I hadn't done so because I was drunk, because I don't get drunk. I'm quite objective about my drinking, know exactly how much liquor I can hold without getting tipsy.

In thinking back over the week the man who called himself Jesus spent at my house, I have to believe he manipulated me into introducing him to my friends. But why? There had been that statement he made about my friends accepting him before I did. They obviously had, but accepted him as what? Surely, none of them were so naive as to think he was the real Jesus. Had they all been in on the plan to screw up my mind? Were they still concocting some big joke against me?

I suppose I really got concerned when Ribs and Blackie didn't show up for their usual Wednesday night meal. I was left with a big bucket of chicken and more jalapeno blackeyed peas than it was humanly possible for one man to eat.

I even attempted to solicit aid and comfort from newfound friend Beep Jenkins, but discovered he had also gravitated to the CHURCH AMONG THE HUBCAPS. I wondered if Beep was finding life among the hubcaps as satisfying as he would have found being a male stripper.

I'm not sure when I first came up with the idea for the birthday party for the man who called himself Jesus. I'm a very giving person, and especially during the Christmas season. I also figured the party could be a tax deduction since there would be some religious connotation to it.

Because of the party, it was necessary for me to go down to the CHURCH AMONG THE HUBCAPS and talk to the man who called himself Jesus. I didn't particularly want to talk to him, but figured he had a right to know I was planning a party in his honor. The party was my way of saying, "Hey, maybe you're who you say you are," though I didn't for one second believe it.

I went down to Chico's early one morning, because I figured that would be the best time to catch the man who called himself Jesus alone. From what I had heard, he was always surrounded by converts, including my alleged friends. With Christmas Day just a couple of days away, it was important to take care of the party details.

Though it was early enough that I hadn't even had my second round of coffee, I found the man who called himself Jesus surrounded by a lot of grubby looking people and some darn nice looking, well-dressed whores. He was talking to these people, but when he saw me he excused himself and came through the door to where I was standing.

"Mark, it's nice to see you," he said, shaking my hand.

"The place looks good," I said. "It's a lot cleaner than it use to be." Everything did seem to have a place, and on my arrival I had noticed that the building had been completely painted. Chico was going to come out okay on this deal.

The man who called himself Jesus laughed and asked, "What brings you to this part of town?"

First, if he was the real Jesus, he would have known why I was there. Second, I had immediately noticed the place didn't even have a church sign on it. Chico's misspelled sign was still the only one on the place. Admittedly, I'm the one who named the place the CHURCH AMONG THE HUBCAPS, but out of respect to me the man could have at least had a sign specifying the place as both a church and a used hubcaps and discount store. In fact, one would think that on a sign CHURCH AMONG THE HUB-CAPS there would also be in smaller letters, *name by Mark Luther.*

But no, I was getting no credit for the contribution I had made to his ministry. It was very unfair.

However, being the gracious and giving person that I am, I said, "With Christmas just a couple of days away, I thought maybe I'd have a birthday party for you."

He chuckled again. "I probably won't be here on my birthday."

"You're leaving before Christmas Day?" I asked.

"I told you my birthday is in the summer."

"The King James Version of the Bible says Jesus was born on Christmas Day," I told him, "and you claim to be Jesus."

"You might want to read that portion of the Bible again," he said.

It was one of his typical ridiculous statements. Once you've read the Bible, you've read it. And there are very few people who can remember and interpret the scripture as well as I can.

"So, you're not interested in having a birthday party?"

"Not really," he said. "I thought maybe you had decided to come down here and help us. We could certainly use your help."

I shrugged my shoulders. "Thanks, but I'm pretty tied up in my own church. I'm planning to attend services Christmas Day."

"That's good," he said, "but you could still come down here and have dinner with us on Christmas Day."

"I'd like to," I said, "but I'm just covered up with invitations for Christmas dinner. I'm surprised, though, that you'd be celebrating Christmas since you claim to be Jesus Christ and say December Twenty-fifth is not your birthday."

"There's nothing wrong in celebrating Christmas Day," he informed, "though in truth, the Christian has reason to celebrate every day. The resurrection is cause for even more celebration."

"Well, I just can't get as festive about Easter as I can about Christmas," I said.

We talked a while longer and then I left.

I overslept and didn't make it to church on Christmas Day. Most of the people who know me thought I was tied up, so I didn't get a dinner invitation. I ate a turkey and dressing TV dinner and watched a couple of games on the tube. It was a nice, quiet day.

XVI

Some people don't know when to end a joke, will take it to extreme limits to prove a point. I'm now more thoroughly convinced than ever that all of my former alleged friends were in on the joke regarding the man who called himself Jesus. You have only to consider what they have done to understand my reasoning.

Mary Lou Magruder is now a missionary to New York, where she is working in a hospice care center. I suggested to Mary Lou that we might try to make a new start, but she wasn't interested.

Jimmy Joe Johnson founded an organization called *Oil Men for Christ,* which is based in West Texas. Jimmy Joe quit selling oil leases and is now spending his time organizing new churches.

Bobo Harrison and his family moved to California. Bobo gave up sports writing and beer and is now a religion writer for one of the major West Coast dailies. He told me there isn't much difference in writing religion and sports.

Billy Bob Raintree is now involved in a prison ministry. Any day now I expect a federal judge to rule that listening to Billy Bob constitutes cruel and unusual punishment.

Joe Don Barnes has founded an organization called *Cops for Christ* and has vowed to single-handedly wipe out drug abuse and alcoholism in the United States. He is so opposed to cigarettes that I may even start smoking.

Bum Criswell has realized his dream of a *Fellowship of Christian Polo Players* organization, and he has been instrumental in founding Christian polo leagues in all fifty states. He is now a circuit polo minister, riding on his trusty steed from polo match to polo match, carrying his message. He is seen on TV quite often, advertising cellular saddle or horse phones.

Bobby Jack Lewis abandoned his dating service business and is now a missionary in darkest Africa. He goes from tribe to tribe, preaching in English to people who have never seen or heard a white man before. The natives think he is charismatic.

Chico Neiman Marcus has not moved from his location on Harry Hines. He still operates his used hubcaps and discount store and preaches to anyone who frequents the place.

Ribs Davis is labeled by some as the greatest Christian accordionist in the world. He has set many hymns to polka music and is a folk hero in Poland. Ribs is often seen and heard on television in this country, and has been referred to by the President as "our greatest weapon against Communism."

Sue Beth Larsen and Chigger Dodgen got married and now have a half dozen kids. Sue Beth started a worldwide organization called *Weight Watchers for Christ* and she has dropped at least a hundred pounds. Chigger in the meantime has not gained an inch in height. For some reason, the Dodgens decided not to pursue their dream of a race track in Highland Park. Sue Beth has given much of her money to charity, and she and Chigger still work with Chico at the CHURCH AMONG THE HUBCAPS.

Beep Jenkins is president of *Coon Hunters for Christ* and has one of the most active whore ministries in the country.

"My daytime job was right there in front of my nose the whole time and I almost didn't see it," Beep told me. "Most of your whores work at night, so they're ripe for some good preaching during the daytime."

While Beep has a big string of whores who support his ministry, he can hardly be called a pastoral pimp.

As for the man who called himself Jesus, I haven't seen or heard from him since the night he told me he was going to leave town. Funny thing, I was sitting on the same barstool where I first met him, nursing a margarita, when he came in to bid me farewell.

"I'll be leaving town tomorrow, so I just wanted to come by and say so long," he said.

I expressed appreciation for his thoughtfulness, then asked, "Where will you be going?"

"I'm going to Oklahoma," he replied.

"Why in the world would you want to go to Oklahoma?"

He laughed. "Maybe it's because I've never been to Oklahoma."